The Poison Eaters and Other Stories

Also by Holly Black

Modern Faerie Tales
Tithe
Valiant
Ironside

The Curse Workers
White Cat
Red Glove (forthcoming)
Black Heart (forthcoming)

The Good Neighbors (with Ted Naifeh)
Kith
Kin
Kind (forthcoming)

Anthologies
Geektastic: Stories of the Nerd Herd, edited by Holly Black and Cecil Castellucci
Zombies vs. Unicorns, edited by Holly Black and Justine Larbalestier (forthcoming)

For Younger Readers

The Spiderwick Chronicles (with Tony DiTerlizzi)
The Field Guide
The Seeing Stone
Lucinda's Secret
The Ironwood Tree
The Wrath of Mulgarath

Beyond the Spiderwick Chronicles (with Tony DiTerlizzi)
The Nixie's Song
A Giant Problem
The Wyrm King

Arthur Spiderwick's Field Guide to the Fantastical World Around You (with Tony DiTerlizzi)
The Care and Feeding of Sprites (with Tony DiTerlizzi)

The Poison Eaters and Other Stories

Holly Black

with illustrations by Theo Black

Big Mouth House
Easthampton, MA

Big Mouth House
150 Pleasant Street #306
Easthampton, MA 01027
www.bigmouthhouse.net
info@bigmouthhouse.net

Distributed to the trade by Consortium.

First Edition
February 2010

Text set in Centaur. Titles set in Kruella.
Printed on 30% post-consumer recycled paper by Thomson-Shore of Dexter, MI.

Library of Congress Cataloging-in-Publication Data available on request.
ISBN 978-1-931520-63-8

Contents

For Steve Berman,
who bullied me into being a better writer
and to whom I will always be grateful.

The Coldest Girl in Coldtown

MATILDA WAS DRUNK, BUT then she was always drunk anymore. Dizzy drunk. Stumbling drunk. Stupid drunk. Whatever kind of drunk she could get.

The man she stood with snaked his hand around her back, warm fingers digging into her side as he pulled her closer. He and his friend with the open-necked shirt grinned down at her like underage equaled dumb, and dumb equaled gullible enough to sleep with them.

She thought they might just be right.

"You want to have a party back at my place?" the man asked. He'd told her his name was Mark, but his friend kept slipping up and calling him by a name that started with a D. Maybe Dan or Dave. They had been smuggling her drinks from the bar whenever they went outside to smoke—drinks mixed sickly sweet that dripped down her throat like candy.

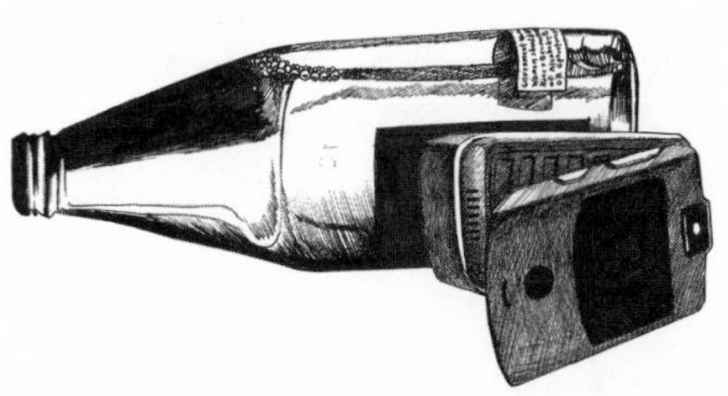

"Sure," she said, grinding her cigarette against the brick wall. She missed the hot ash in her hand, but concentrated on the alcoholic numbness turning her limbs to lead. Smiled. "Can we pick up more beer?"

They exchanged an obnoxious glance she pretended not to notice. The friend—he called himself Ben—looked at her glassy eyes and her cold-flushed cheeks. Her sloppy hair. He probably made guesses about a troubled home life. She hoped so.

"You're not going to get sick on us?" he asked. Just out of the hot bar, beads of sweat had collected in the hollow of his throat. The skin shimmered with each swallow.

She shook her head to stop staring. "I'm barely tipsy," she lied.

"I've got plenty of stuff back at my place," said MarkDanDave. *Mardave,* Matilda thought and giggled.

"Buy me a 40," she said. She knew it was stupid to go with them, but it was even stupider if she sobered up. "One of those wine coolers. They have them at the bodega on the corner. Otherwise, no party."

Both of the guys laughed. She tried to laugh with them even though she knew she wasn't included in the joke. She was the joke. The trashy little slut. The girl who can be bought for a big fat wine cooler and three cranberry-and-vodkas.

"Okay, okay," said Mardave.

They walked down the street and she found herself leaning easily into the heat of their bodies, inhaling the sweat and iron scent. It would be easy for her to close her eyes and pretend Mardave was someone else, someone she wanted to be touched by, but she wouldn't let herself soil her memories of Julian.

They passed by a store with flat-screens in the window, each one showing different channels. One streamed video from Coldtown—a girl who went by the name Demonia made some kind of deal with one of the stations to show what it was really like behind the gates. She filmed the Eternal Ball, a party that started in 1998 and had gone on ceaselessly ever since. In the background, girls and boys in rubber harnesses swung through the air. They stopped occasionally, opening what looked like a modded hospital tube stuck on the inside of their arms just below the crook of the elbow. They twisted a knob and spilled blood into little paper cups for the partygoers. A boy who looked to be about nine, wearing a string of glowing beads around his neck, gulped down the contents of one of the cups and then licked the paper with a tongue as red as his eyes. The camera angle changed suddenly, veering up, and the viewers saw the domed top of the hall, full of cracked windows through which you could glimpse the stars.

"I know where they are," Mardave said. "I can see that building from my apartment."

"Aren't you scared of living so close to the vampires?" she asked, a small smile pulling at the corners of her mouth.

"We'll protect you," said Ben, smiling back at her.

"We should do what other countries do and blow those corpses sky high," Mardave said.

Matilda bit her tongue not to point out that Europe's vampire hunting led to the highest levels of infection in the world. So many of Belgium's citizens were vampires that shops barely opened their doors until nightfall. The truce with Coldtown worked. Mostly.

She didn't care if Mardave hated vampires. She hated them too.

When they got to the store, she waited outside to avoid getting carded and lit another cigarette with Julian's silver lighter—the one she was going to give back to him in thirty-one days. Sitting down on the curb, she let the chill of the pavement deaden the backs of her thighs. Let it freeze her belly and frost her throat with ice that even liquor couldn't melt.

Hunger turned her stomach. She couldn't remember the last time she'd eaten anything solid without throwing it back up. Her mouth hungered for dark, rich feasts; her skin felt tight, like a seed thirsting to bloom. All she could trust herself to eat was smoke.

When she was a little girl, vampires had been costumes for Halloween. They were the bad guys in movies, plastic fangs and polyester capes. They were Muppets on television, endlessly counting.

Now she was the one who was counting. Fifty-seven days. Eighty-eight days. Eighty-eight nights.

"Matilda?"

She looked up and saw Dante saunter up to her, earbuds dangling out of his ears like he needed a soundtrack for everything he did. He wore a pair of skintight jeans and smoked a cigarette out of one of those long, movie-star holders. He looked pretentious as hell. "I'd almost given up on finding you."

"You should have started with the gutter," she said, gesturing to the wet, clogged tide beneath her feet. "I take my gutter-dwelling very seriously."

"*Seriously.*" He pointed at her with the cigarette holder. "Even your mother thinks you're dead. Julian's crying over you."

Maltilda looked down and picked at the thread of her jeans.

It hurt to think about Julian while waiting for Mardave and Ben. She was disgusted with herself, and she could only guess how disgusted he'd be. "I got Cold," she said. "One of them bit me."

Dante nodded his head.

That's what they'd started calling it when the infection kicked in—Cold—because of how cold people's skin became after they were bitten. And because of the way the poison in their veins caused them to crave heat and blood. One taste of human blood and the infection mutated. It killed the host and then raised it back up again, colder than before. Cold through and through, forever and ever.

"I didn't think you'd be alive," he said.

She hadn't thought she'd make it this long either without giving in. But going it alone on the street was better than forcing her mother to choose between chaining her up in the basement or shipping her off to Coldtown. It was better, too, than taking the chance Matilda might get loose from the chains and attack people she loved. Stories like that were in the news all the time; almost as frequent as the ones about people who let vampires into their homes because they seemed so nice and clean-cut.

"Then what are you doing looking for me?" she asked. Dante had lived down the street from her family for years, but they didn't hang out. She'd wave to him as she mowed the lawn while he loaded his panel van with DJ equipment. He shouldn't have been here.

She looked back at the store window. Mardave and Ben were at the counter with a case of beer and her wine cooler. They were getting change from a clerk.

"I was hoping you, er, *wouldn't* be alive," Dante said. "You'd be more help if you were dead."

She stood up, stumbling slightly. "Well, screw you too."

It took eighty-eight days for the venom to sweat out a person's pores. She only had thirty-seven to go. Thirty-seven days to stay so drunk that she could ignore the buzz in her head that made her want to bite, rend, devour.

"That came out wrong," he said, taking a step toward her. Close enough that she felt the warmth of him radiating off him like licking tongues of flame. She shivered. Her veins sang with need.

"I can't help you," said Matilda. "Look, I can barely help myself. Whatever it is, I'm sorry. I can't. You have to get out of here."

"My sister Lydia and your boyfriend Julian are gone," Dante said. "Together. She's looking to get bitten. I don't know what he's looking for . . . but he's going to get hurt."

Matilda gaped at him as Mardave and Ben walked out of the store. Ben carried a box on his shoulder and a bag on his arm. "That guy bothering you?" he asked her.

"No," she said, then turned to Dante. "You better go."

"Wait," said Dante.

Matilda's stomach hurt. She was sobering up. The smell of blood seemed to float up from underneath their skin.

She reached into Ben's bag and grabbed a beer. She popped the top, licked off the foam. If she didn't get a lot drunker, she was going to attack someone.

"Jesus," Mardave said. "Slow down. What if someone sees you?"

She drank it in huge gulps, right there on the street. Ben laughed, but it wasn't a good laugh. He was laughing at the drunk.

"She's infected," Dante said.

Matilda whirled toward him, chucking the mostly empty can in his direction automatically. "Shut up, asshole."

"Feel her skin," Dante said. "Cold. She ran away from home when it happened, and no one's seen her since."

"I'm cold because it's cold out," she said.

She saw Ben's evaluation of her change from *damaged enough to sleep with strangers* to *dangerous enough to attack strangers.*

Mardave touched his hand gently to her arm. "Hey," he said.

She almost hissed with delight at the press of his hot fingers. She smiled up at him and hoped her eyes weren't as hungry as her skin. "I really like you."

He flinched. "Look, it's late. Maybe we could meet up another time." Then he backed away, which made her so angry that she bit the inside of her own cheek.

Her mouth flooded with the taste of copper and a red haze floated in front of her eyes.

Fifty-seven days ago, Matilda had been sober. She'd had a boyfriend named Julian, and they would dress up together in her bedroom. He liked to wear skinny ties and glittery eye shadow. She liked to wear vintage rock t-shirts and boots that laced up so high that they would constantly be late because they were busy tying them.

Matilda and Julian would dress up and prowl the streets and party at lockdown clubs that barred the doors from dusk to dawn. Matilda wasn't particularly careless; she was just careless enough.

She'd been at a friend's party. It had been stiflingly hot, and she was mad because Julian and Lydia were doing some dance thing from the musical they were in at school. Matilda just wanted to get some air. She opened a window and climbed out under the bobbing garland of garlic.

Another girl was already on the lawn. Matilda should have noticed that the girl's breath didn't crystallize in the air, but she didn't.

"Do you have a light?" the girl had asked.

Matilda did. She reached for Julian's lighter when the girl caught her arm and bent her backwards. Matilda's scream turned into a shocked cry when she felt the girl's cold mouth against her neck, the girl's cold fingers holding her off balance.

Then it was as though someone slid two shards of ice into her skin.

The spread of vampirism could be traced to one person—Caspar Morales. Films and books and television had started romanticizing vampires, and maybe it was only a matter of time before a vampire started romanticizing *himself*.

Crazy, romantic Caspar decided that he wouldn't kill his victims. He'd just drink a little blood and then move on, city to city. By the time other vampires caught up with him and ripped him to pieces, he'd infected hundreds of people. And those new vampires, with no idea how to prevent the spread, infected thousands.

When the first outbreak happened in Tokyo, it seemed like a journalist's prank. Then there was another outbreak in Hong Kong and another in San Francisco.

The military put up barricades around the area where the infection broke out. That was the way the first Coldtown was founded.

Matilda's body twitched involuntarily. She could feel the spasm start in the muscles of her back and move to her face. She wrapped her arms around herself to try and stop it, but her hands were shaking pretty hard. "You want my help, you better get me some booze."

"You're killing yourself," Dante said, shaking his head.

"I just need another drink," she said. "Then I'll be fine."

He shook his head. "You can't keep going like this. You can't just stay drunk to avoid your problems. I know, people do. It's a classic move, even, but I didn't figure you for fetishizing your own doom."

She started laughing. "You don't understand. When I'm wasted I don't crave blood. It's the only thing keeping me human."

"What?" He looked at Matilda like he couldn't quite make sense of her words.

"Let me spell it out: if you don't get me some alcohol, I am going to bite you."

"Oh." He fumbled for his wallet. "Oh. Okay."

Matilda had spent all the cash she'd brought with her in the first few weeks, so it'd been a long time since she could simply overpay some homeless guy to go into a liquor store and get her a fifth of vodka. She gulped gratefully from the bottle Dante gave her in a nearby alley.

A few moments later, warmth started to creep up from her belly, and her mouth felt like it was full of needles and Novocain.

"You okay?" he asked her.

"Better now," she said, her words slurring slightly. "But I still don't understand. Why do you need me to help you find Lydia and Julian?

"Lydia got obsessed with becoming a vampire," Dante said, irritably brushing back the stray hair that fell across his face.

"Why?"

He shrugged. "She used to be really scared of vampires. When we were kids, she begged Mom to let her camp in the hallway because she wanted to sleep where there were no windows. But then I guess she started to be fascinated instead. She thinks that human annihilation is coming. She says that we all have to choose sides and she's already chosen."

"I'm not a vampire," Matilda said.

Dante gestured irritably with his cigarette holder. The cigarette had long burned out. He didn't look like his usual contemptuous self; he looked lost. "I know. I thought you would be. And—I don't know—you're on the street. Maybe you know more than the video feeds do about where someone might go to get themselves bitten."

Matilda thought about lying on the floor of Julian's parents' living room. They had been sweaty from dancing and kissed languidly. On the television, a list of missing people flashed. She had closed her eyes and kissed him again.

She nodded slowly. "I know a couple of places. Have you heard from her at all?"

He shook his head. "She won't take any of my calls, but she's been updating her blog. I'll show you."

He loaded it on his phone. The latest entry was titled: *I Need a Vampire.* Matilda scrolled down and read. Basically, it was Lydia's plea to be bitten. She wanted any vampires looking for victims to contact her. In the comments, someone suggested Coldtown and then another person commented in ALL CAPS to say that everyone knew that the vampires in Coldtown were careful to keep their food sources alive.

It was impossible to know which comments Lydia had read and which ones she believed.

Runaways went to Coldtown all the time, along with the sick, the sad, and the maudlin. There was supposed to be a constant party, theirs for the price of blood. But once they went inside, humans—even human children, even babies born in Coldtown—weren't be allowed to leave. The National Guard patrolled the barbed wire–wrapped and garlic-covered walls to make sure that Coldtown stayed contained.

People said that vampires found ways through the walls to the outside world. Maybe that was just a rumor, although Matilda remembered reading something online about a documentary that proved the truth. She hadn't seen it.

But everyone knew there was only one way to get out of Coldtown if you were still human. Your family had to be rich enough to hire a vampire hunter. Vampire hunters got money from the government for each vampire they put in Coldtown, but they could give up the cash reward in favor of a voucher for a single human's release. One vampire in, one human out.

There was a popular reality television series about one of the hunters, called *Hemlok*. Girls hung posters of him on the insides of their lockers, often right next to pictures of the vampires he hunted.

Most people didn't have the money to outbid the government for a hunter's services. Matilda didn't think that Dante's family did and knew Julian's didn't. Her only chance was to catch Lydia and Julian before they crossed over.

"What's with Julian?" Matilda asked. She'd been avoiding the question for hours as they walked through the alleys that grew progressively more empty the closer they got to the gates.

"What do you mean?" Dante was hunched over against the wind, his long skinny frame offering little protection against the chill. Still, she knew he was warm underneath. Inside.

"Why did Julian go with her?" She tried to keep the hurt out of her voice. She didn't think Dante would understand. He DJed at a club in town and was rumored to see a different boy or girl every day of the week. The only person he actually seemed to care about was his sister.

Dante shrugged slim shoulders. "Maybe he was looking for you."

That was the answer she wanted to hear. She smiled and let herself imagine saving Julian right before he could enter Coldtown. He would tell her that he'd been coming to save her and then they'd laugh and she wouldn't bite him, no matter how warm his skin felt.

Dante snapped his fingers in front of Matilda and she stumbled.

"Hey," she said. "Drunk girl here. No messing with me."

He chuckled.

Melinda and Dante checked all the places she knew, all the places she'd slept on cardboard near runaways and begged for change. Dante had a picture of Lydia in his wallet, but no one who looked at it remembered her.

Finally, outside a bar, they bumped into a girl who said she'd seen Lydia and Julian. Dante traded her the rest of his pack of cigarettes for her story.

"They were headed for Coldtown," she said, lighting up. In the flickering flame of her lighter, Melinda noticed the shallow cuts along her wrists. "Said she was tired of waiting."

"What about the guy?" Matilda asked. She stared at the girl's dried garnet scabs. They looked like crusts of sugar, like the lines of salt left on the beach when the tide goes out. She wanted to lick them.

"He said his girlfriend was a vampire," said the girl, inhaling deeply. She blew out smoke and then started to cough.

"When was that?" Dante asked.

The girl shrugged her shoulders. "Just a couple of hours ago."

Dante took out his phone and pressed some buttons. "Load," he muttered. "Come on, *load*."

"What happened to your arms?" Matilda asked.

The girl shrugged again. "They bought some blood off me.

Said that they might need it inside. They had a real professional set-up too. Sharp razor and one of those glass bowls with the plastic lids."

Matilda's stomach clenched with hunger. She turned against the wall and breathed slowly. She needed a drink.

"Is something wrong with her?" the girl asked.

"Matilda," Dante said, and Matilda half-turned. He was holding out his phone. There was a new entry up on Lydia's blog, entitled: *One-Way Ticket to Coldtown.*

"You should post about it," Dante said. "On the message boards."

Matilda was sitting on the ground, picking at the brick wall to give her fingers something to do. Dante had massively overpaid for another bottle of vodka and was cradling it in a crinkled paper bag.

She frowned. "Post about what?"

"About the alcohol. About it helping you keep from turning."

"Where would I post about that?"

Dante twisted off the cap. The heat seemed to radiate off his skin as he swigged from the bottle. "There are forums for people who have to restrain someone for eighty-eight days. They hang out and exchange tips on straps and dealing with the begging for blood. Haven't you seen them?"

She shook her head. "I bet sedation's already a hot topic of discussion. I doubt I'd be telling them anything they don't already know"

He laughed, but it was a bitter laugh. "Then there's all the people who want to be vampires. The websites reminding all the corpsebait out there that being bitten by an infected person isn't enough; it has to be a vampire. The ones listing gimmicks to get vampires to notice you."

"Like what?"

"I dated a girl who cut thin lines on her thighs before she went out dancing so if there was a vampire in the club, it'd be drawn to her scent." Dante didn't look extravagant or affected anymore. He looked defeated.

Matilda smiled at him. "She was probably a better bet than me for getting you into Coldtown."

He returned the smile wanly. "The worst part is that Lydia's not going to get what she wants. She's going become the human servant of some vampire who's going to make her a whole bunch of promises and never turn her. The last thing they need in Coldtown is new vampires."

Matilda imagined Lydia and Julian dancing at the endless Eternal Ball. She pictured them on the streets she'd seen in pictures uploaded to Facebook and Flickr, trying to trade a bowl full of blood for their own deaths.

When Dante passed the bottle to her, she pretended to swig. On the eve of her fifty-eighth day of being infected, Matilda started sobering up.

Crawling over, she straddled Dante's waist before he had a chance to shift positions. His mouth tasted like tobacco. When she pulled back from him, his eyes were wide with surprise, his pupils blown and black even in the dim streetlight.

"Matilda," he said and there was nothing in his voice but longing.

"If you really want your sister, I am going to need one more thing from you," she said.

His blood tasted like tears.

Matilda's skin felt like it had caught fire. She'd turned into lit paper, burning up. Curling into black ash.

She licked his neck over and over and over.

The gates of Coldtown were large and made of consecrated wood, barbed wire covering them like heavy, thorny vines. The guards slouched at their posts, guns over their shoulders, sharing a cigarette. The smell of percolating coffee wafted out of the guardhouse.

"Um, hello," Matilda said. Blood was still sticky where it half-dried around her mouth and on her neck. It had dribbled down her shirt, stiffening it nearly to cracking when she moved. Her body felt strange now that she was dying. Hot. More alive than it had in weeks.

Dante would be all right; she wasn't contagious and she didn't think she'd hurt him too badly. She hoped she hadn't hurt him too badly. She touched the phone in her pocket, his phone, the one she'd used to call 911 after she'd left him.

"Hello," she called to the guards again.

One turned. "Oh my god," he said and reached for his rifle.

"I'm here to turn in a vampire. For a voucher. I want to turn in a vampire in exchange for letting a human out of Coldtown."

"What vampire?" asked the other guard. He'd dropped the

cigarette, but not stepped on the filter so that it just smoked on the asphalt.

"Me," said Matilda. "I want to turn in me."

They made her wait as her pulse thrummed slower and slower. She wasn't a vampire yet, and after a few phone calls, they discovered that technically she could only have the voucher after undeath. They did let her wash her face in the bathroom of the guardhouse and wring the thin cloth of her shirt until the water ran down the drain clear, instead of murky with blood.

When she looked into the mirror, her skin had unfamiliar purple shadows, like bruises. She was still staring at them when she stopped being able to catch her breath. The hollow feeling in her chest expanded and she found herself panicked, falling to her knees on the filthy tile floor. She died there, a moment later.

It didn't hurt as much as she'd worried it would. Like most things, the surprise was the worst part.

The guards released Matilda into Coldtown just a little before dawn. The world looked strange—everything had taken on a smudgy, silvery cast, like she was watching an old movie. Sometimes people's heads seemed to blur into black smears. Only one color was distinct—a pulsing, oozing color that seemed to glow from beneath skin.

Red.

Her teeth ached to look at it.

There was a silence inside her. No longer did she move to the rhythmic drumming of her heart. Her body felt strange, hard as marble, free of pain. She'd never realized how many small agonies were alive in the creak of her bones, the pull of muscle. Now, free of them, she felt like she was floating.

Matilda looked around with her strange new eyes. Everything was beautiful. And the light at the edge of the sky was the most beautiful thing of all.

"What are you doing?" a girl called from a doorway. She had long black hair, but her roots were growing in blonde. "Get in here! Are you crazy?"

In a daze, Matilda did as she was told. Everything smeared as she moved, like the world was painted in watercolors. The girl's pinkish-red face swirled along with it.

It was obvious the house had once been grand, but it looked like it'd been abandoned for a long time. Graffiti covered the peeling wallpaper and couches had been pushed up against the walls. A boy wearing jeans but no shirt was painting make-up onto a girl with stiff pink pigtails, while another girl in a retro polka-dotted dress pulled on mesh stockings.

In a corner, another boy—this one with glossy brown hair that fell to his waist—stacked jars of creamed corn into a precarious pyramid.

"What is this place?" Matilda asked.

The boy stacking the jars turned. "Look at her eyes. She's a vampire!" He didn't seem afraid, though; he seemed delighted.

"Get her into the cellar," one of the other girls said.

"Come on," said the black-haired girl and pulled Matilda toward a doorway. "You're fresh-made, right?"

"Yeah," Matilda said. Her tongue swept over her own sharp teeth. "I guess that's pretty obvious."

"Don't you know that vampires can't go outside in the daylight?" the girl asked, shaking her head. "The guards try that trick with every new vampire, but I never saw one almost fall for it."

"Oh, right," Matilda said. They went down the rickety steps to a filthy basement with a mattress on the floor underneath a single bulb. Crates of foodstuffs were shoved against the walls, and the high, small windows had been painted over with a tarry substance that let no light through.

The black-haired girl who'd waved her inside smiled. "We trade with the border guards. Black-market food, clothes, little luxuries like chocolate and cigarettes for some ass. Vampires don't own everything."

"And you're going to owe us for letting you stay the night," the boy said from the top of the stairs.

"I don't have anything," Matilda said. "I didn't bring any cans of food or whatever."

"You have to bite us."

"What?" Matilda asked.

"One of us," the girl said. "How about one of us? You can even pick which one."

"Why would you want me to do that?"

The girl's expression clearly said that Matilda was stupid. "Who doesn't want to live forever?"

I don't, Matilda wanted to say, but she swallowed the words. She could tell they already thought she didn't deserve to be a vampire. Besides, she wanted to taste blood. She wanted to taste the red, throbbing, pulsing insides of the girl in front of her. It wasn't the pain she'd felt when she was infected, the hunger that made her stomach clench, the craving for warmth. It was heady, greedy desire.

"Tomorrow," Matilda said. "When it's night again."

"Okay," the girl said, "but you promise, right? You'll turn one of us?"

"Yeah," said Matilda, numbly. It was hard to even wait that long.

She was relieved when they went upstairs, but less relieved when she heard something heavy slide in front of the basement door. She told herself that didn't matter. The only thing that mattered was getting through the day so that she could find Julian and Lydia.

She shook her head to clear it of thoughts of blood and turned on Dante's phone. Although she didn't expect it, a text message was waiting: *I cant tell if I luv u or if I want to kill u.*

Relief washed over her. Her mouth twisted into a smile and her newly sharp canines cut her lip. She winced. Dante was okay.

She opened up Lydia's blog and posted an anonymous message: *Tell Julian his girlfriend wants to see him . . . and you.*

Matilda made herself comfortable on the dirty mattress. She looked up at the rotted boards of the ceiling and thought of Julian. She had a single ticket out of Coldtown and two humans to rescue with it, but it was easy to picture herself saving Lydia as Julian valiantly offered to stay with her, even promised her his eternal devotion.

She licked her lips at the image. When she closed her eyes, all her imaginings drowned in a sea of red.

Waking at dusk, Matilda checked Lydia's blog. Lydia had posted a reply: *Meet us at the Festival of Sinners.*

Five kids sat at the top of the stairs, watching her with liquid eyes.

"Are you awake?" the black-haired girl asked. She seemed to pulse with color. Her moving mouth was hypnotic.

"Come here," Matilda said to her in a voice that seemed so distant that she was surprised to find it was her own. She hadn't meant to speak, hadn't meant to beckon the girl over to her.

"That's not fair," one of the boys called. "I was the one who said she owed us something. It should be me. You should pick me."

Matilda ignored him as the girl knelt down on the dirty mattress and swept aside her hair, baring a long, unmarked neck. She seemed dazzling, this creature of blood and breath, a fragile manikin as brittle as sticks.

Tiny golden hairs tickled Matilda's nose as she bit down.

And gulped.

Blood was heat and heart running-thrumming-beating through the fat roots of veins to drip syrup slow, spurting molten hot across tongue, mouth, teeth, chin.

Dimly, Matilda felt someone shoving her and someone else screaming, but it seemed distant and unimportant. Eventually the words became clearer.

"Stop," someone was screaming. "Stop!"

Hands dragged Matilda off the girl. Her neck was a glistening red mess. Gore stained the mattress and covered Matilda's hands and hair. The girl coughed, blood bubbles frothing on her lip, and then went abruptly silent.

"What did you do?" the boy wailed, cradling the girl's body. "She's dead. She's dead. You killed her."

Matilda backed away from the body. Her hand went automatically to her mouth, covering it. "I didn't mean to," she said.

"Maybe she'll be okay," said the other boy, his voice cracking. "We have to get bandages."

"She's *dead*," the boy holding the girl's body moaned.

A thin wail came from deep inside Matilda as she backed toward the stairs. Her belly felt full, distended. She wanted to be sick.

Another girl grabbed Matilda's arm. "Wait," the girl said, eyes wide and imploring. "You have to bite me next. You're full now so you won't have to hurt me—"

With a cry, Matilda tore herself free and ran up the stairs—if she went fast enough, maybe she could escape from herself.

By the time Matilda got to the Festival of Sinners, her mouth tasted metallic and she was numb with fear. She wasn't human, wasn't good, and wasn't sure what she might do next. She kept pawing at her shirt, as if that much blood could ever be wiped off, as if it hadn't already soaked down into her skin and her soiled insides.

The Festival was easy to find, even as confused as she was. People were happy to give her directions, apparently not bothered that she was drenched in blood. Their casual demeanor was horrifying, but not as horrifying as how much she already wanted to feed again.

On the way, she passed the Eternal Ball. Strobe lights lit up the remains of the windows along the dome, and a girl with blue hair in a dozen braids held up a video camera to interview three men dressed all in white with gleaming red eyes.

Vampires.

A ripple of fear passed through her. She reminded herself that there was nothing they could do to her. She was already like them. Already dead.

The Festival of Sinners was being held at a church with stained-glass windows painted black on the inside. The door, papered with pink-stenciled posters, was painted the same thick tarry black. Music thrummed from within and a few people sat on the steps, smoking and talking.

Matilda went inside.

A doorman pulled aside a velvet rope for her, letting her past a small line of people waiting to pay the cover charge. The rules were different for vampires, perhaps especially for vampires accessorizing their grungy attire with so much blood.

Matilda scanned the room. She didn't see Julian or Lydia, just a throng of dancers and a bar that served alcohol from vast copper distilling vats. It spilled into mismatched mugs. Then one of the people near the bar moved and Matilda saw Lydia and Julian. He was bending over her, shouting into her ear.

Matilda pushed her way through the crowd, until she was close enough to touch Julian's arm. She reached out, but couldn't quite bring herself to brush his skin with her foulness.

Julian looked up, startled. "Tilda?"

She snatched back her hand like she'd been about to touch fire.

"Tilda," he said. "What happened to you? Are you hurt?"

Matilda flinched, looking down at herself. "I . . ."

Lydia laughed. "She ate someone, moron."

"Tilda?" Julian asked.

"I'm sorry," Matilda said. There was so much she had to be sorry for, but at least he was here now. Julian would tell her what to do and how to turn herself back into something decent again. She would save Lydia and Julian would save her.

He touched her shoulder, let his hand rest gingerly on her blood-stiffened shirt. "We were looking for you everywhere." His gentle expression was tinged with terror; fear pulled his smile into something closer to a grimace.

"I wasn't in Coldtown," Matilda said. "I came here so that Lydia could leave. I have a pass."

"But I don't want to leave," said Lydia. "You understand that, right? I want what you have—eternal life."

"You're not infected," Matilda said. "You have to go. You can still be okay. Please, I need you to go."

"One pass?" Julian said, his eyes going to Lydia. Matilda saw the truth in the weight of that gaze—Julian had not come to Coldtown for Matilda. Even though she knew she didn't deserve him to think of her as anything but a monster, it hurt savagely.

"I'm not leaving," Lydia said, turning to Julian, pouting. "You said she wouldn't be like this."

"*I killed a girl,*" Matilda said. "I killed her. Do you understand that?"

"Who cares about some mortal girl?" Lydia tossed back her hair. In that moment, she reminded Matilda of her brother, pretentious Dante who'd turned out to be an actual nice guy. Just like sweet Lydia had turned out cruel.

"You're a girl," Matilda said. "You're mortal."

"I know that!" Lydia rolled her eyes. "I just mean that we don't care who you killed. Turn us and then we can kill lots of people."

"No," Matilda said, swallowing. She looked down, not wanting to hear what she was about to say. There was still a chance. "Look, I have the pass. If you don't want it, then Julian should take it and go. But I'm not turning you. I'm never turning you, understand."

"Julian doesn't want to leave," Lydia said. Her eyes looked bright and two feverish spots appeared on her cheeks. "Who are you to judge me anyway? You're the murderer."

Matilda took a step back. She desperately wanted Julian to say something in her defense or even to look at her, but his gaze remained steadfastly on Lydia.

"So neither one of you want the pass," Matilda said.

"Fuck you," spat Lydia.

Matilda turned away.

"Wait," Julian said. His voice sounded weak.

Matilda spun, unable to keep the hope off her face, and saw why Julian had called to her. Lydia stood behind him, a long knife to his throat.

"Turn me," Lydia said. "Turn me, or I'm going to kill him."

Julian's eyes were wide. He started to protest or beg or something and Lydia pressed the knife harder, silencing him.

People had stopped dancing nearby, backing away. One girl with red-glazed eyes stared hungrily at the knife.

"Turn me!" Lydia shouted. "I'm tired of waiting! I want my life to begin!"

"You won't be alive—" Matilda started.

"I'll be alive—more alive than ever. Just like you are."

"Okay," Matilda said softly. "Give me your wrist."

The crowd seemed to close in tighter, watching as Lydia held out her arm. Matilda crouched low, bending down over it.

"Take the knife away from his throat," Matilda said.

Lydia, all her attention on Matilda, let Julian go. He stumbled a little and pressed his fingers to his neck.

"I loved you," Julian shouted.

Matilda looked up to see that he wasn't speaking to her. She gave him a glittering smile and bit down on Lydia's wrist.

The girl screamed, but the scream was lost in Matilda's ears. Lost in the pulse of blood, the tide of gluttonous pleasure and the music throbbing around them like Lydia's slowing heartbeat.

Matilda sat on the blood-soaked mattress and turned on the video camera to check that the live feed was working.

Julian was gone. She'd given him the pass after stripping him of all his cash and credit cards; there was no point in trying to force Lydia to leave since she'd just come right back in. He'd made stammering apologies that Matilda ignored; then he fled for the gate. She didn't miss him. Her fantasy of Julian felt as ephemeral as her old life.

"It's working," one of the boys—Michael—said from the stairs, a computer cradled on his lap. Even though she'd killed one of them, they welcomed her back, eager enough for eternal life to risk more deaths. "You're streaming live video."

Matilda set the camera on the stack of crates, pointed toward her and the wall where she'd tied a gagged Lydia. The girl thrashed and kicked, but Matilda ignored her. She stepped in front of the camera and smiled.

My name is Matilda Green. I was born on April 10, 1997. I died on September 3, 2013. Please tell my mother I'm okay. And Dante, if you're watching this, I'm sorry.

You've probably seen lots of video feeds from inside Coldtown. I saw them too. Pictures of girls and boys grinding together in clubs or bleeding elegantly for their celebrity vampire masters. Here's what you never see. What I'm going to show you.

For eighty-eight days you are going to watch someone sweat out the infection. You are going to watch her beg and scream and cry. You're going to watch her throw up food and piss her pants and pass out. You're going to watch me feed her can after can of creamed corn. It's not going to be pretty.

You're going to watch me, too. I'm the kind of vampire that you'd be, one who's new at this and basically out of control. I've already killed someone and I can't guarantee I'm not going to do it again. I'm the one who infected this girl.

This is the real Coldtown.

I'm the real Coldtown.

You still want in?

A Reversal of Fortune

NIKKI OPENED THE REFRIGERATOR. There was nothing in there but a couple of shriveled oranges and three gallons of tap water. She slammed it closed. Summer was supposed to be the best part of the year, but so far Nikki's summer sucked. It sucked hard. It sucked like a vacuum that got hold of the drapes.

Her pit bull, Boo, whined and scraped at the door, etching new lines into the frayed wood. Nikki clipped on his leash. She knew she should trim his nails. They frayed the nylon of his collar and gouged the door, but when she tried to cut them, he cried like a baby. Nikki figured he'd had enough pain in his life and left his nails long.

"Come on, Boo," she said as she led him out the front door of the trailer. The air outside shimmered with heat and the air conditioner chugged away in the window, dribbling water down the aluminum siding.

Lifting the lid of the rusty mailbox, Nikki pulled out a handful of circulars and bills. There, among them, she found a stale half-bagel with the words "Butter me!" written on it in gel pen and the crumbly surface stamped with half a dozen stamps. She sighed. Renee's crazy postcards had stopped making her laugh.

Boo hopped down the cement steps gingerly, paws smearing sour-cherry tree pulp and staining his feet purple. He paused when he hit their tiny patch of sun-withered lawn to lick one of the hairless scars along his back.

"Come *on.* I have to get ready for work." Nikki gave his collar a sharp tug.

He yelped and she felt instantly terrible. He'd put on some weight since she'd found him, but he still was pretty easily freaked. She leaned down to pat the solid warmth of his back. His tail started going and he turned his massive face and licked her cheek.

Of course that was the moment her neighbor, Trevor, drove up in his gleaming black truck. He parked in front of his trailer and hopped out, the plastic connective tissue of a six-pack threaded between his fingers. She admired the way the muscles on his back moved as he walked to the door of his place, making the raven tattoo on his shoulder ripple.

"Hey," she called, pushing Boo's wet face away and standing up. Why did Trevor pick this moment to be around, when she was covered in dog drool, hair in tangles, wearing her brother's gi-normous t-shirt? Even the thong on one of her flip-flops had ripped out so she shuffled to keep the sole on.

The dog raised his leg and pissed on a dandelion just as Trevor turned around and gave her a negligent half-wave.

Boo rooted around for a few minutes more and then Nikki tugged him inside. She pulled on a pair of low-slung orange pants and a black T-shirt with the outline of a daschund on it. Busy thinking of Trevor, she stepped onto the asphalt of the self-service car wash—almost to the bus stop—before she realized she still wore her broken flip-flops.

Sighing, she started to wade through the streams of antifreeze-green cleanser and gobs of snowy foam bubbles. They mixed with the sour-cherry spatter that fell from the trees to make the summers smell like a chemical plant of rotten fruit.

There were only a couple of people waiting on the bench, the stink of exhaust from the highway not appearing to bother them one bit. Two women with oversized glasses were chatting away, their curled hair wilting in the heat. An elderly man in a black and white houndstooth suit leaned on a cane and grinned when she got closer.

Just then, Nikki's brother Doug's battered grey Honda pulled into the trailer park. He headed for the back—the best place to park even though you sometimes got a ticket. Her brother anticipated a big winning in another month and seemed to think he was already made of money.

Nikki ran over to the car and rapped on the window.

Doug jumped in his seat, then scowled when he saw her. His beard glimmered with grease as he eased himself out of the car. He was a big guy to begin with and more than four hundred pounds now. Nikki was just the opposite—skinny as a straw no matter what she ate.

"Can you take me to work?" she asked. "It's too hot to take the bus."

He shook his head and belched, making the air smell like a beach after the tide went out and left the mussels to bake in the sun. "I got some more training to do. Spinks is coming over to do gallon-water trials."

"Come on," she said. It sucked that he got to screw around when she had to work. "Where were you anyway?"

"Chinese buffet," he said. "Did fifty shrimp. Volume's okay, I guess. My speed blows, though. I just slow down after the first five to eight minutes. Peeling is a bitch, and those waitresses are always looking at me and giggling."

"Take me to work. You are going to puke if you eat anything else."

His eyes widened and he held up a hand, as if to ward off her words. "How many times do I have to tell you? It's a 'reversal of fortune' or a 'Roman incident.' Don't *ever* say puke. That's bad luck."

Nikki shifted her weight, the intensity of his reaction embarrassing her. "Fine. Whatever. Sorry."

He sighed. "I'll drive you, but you have to take the bus home."

She sat down in one of the cracked seats of his car, brushing off a tangle of silvery wrappers. A pack of gum sat in the grimy brake well and she pulled out a piece. "Deal."

"Good for jaw strength," Doug said.

"Good for fresh breath," she replied, rolling her eyes. "Not that you care about that."

He looked out the window. "Gurgitators get groupies, you know. Once I'm established on the competitive eating circuit, I'll be meeting tons of women."

"There's a scary thought," she said as they pulled onto the highway.

"You should try it. I'm battling the whole 'belt of fat'

thing—my stomach only expands so far—but the skinny people can really pack it in. You should see this little girl who's eating big guys like me under the table."

"If you keep emptying out the fridge, I might just do it," Nikki said. "I might have to."

Nikki walked through the crowded mall, past skaters getting kicked out by rent-a-cops and listless homemakers pushing baby carriages. At the beginning of summer, when she'd first gotten the job, she had imagined that Renee would still be working at the t-shirt kiosk and Leah would be at Gotheteria and they would wave to each other across the body of the mall and go to the food court every day for lunch. She didn't expect that Renee would be on some extended road-trip vacation with her parents and that Leah would ignore Nikki in front of her new, black-lipsticked friends.

If not for Boo, she would spent the summer waiting around for the bizarre postcards Renee sent from cross-country stops. At first they were just pictures of the Liberty Bell or the Smithsonian with messages on the back about the cute guys she'd seen at a rest stop or the number of times she'd punched her brother using the excuse of playing Padiddle—but then they started to get loonier. A museum brochure where Renee had given each of the paintings obscene thought balloons. A ripped piece of a menu with words blacked out to spell messages like "Cheese is the way." A leaf that got too mangled in the mail to read the words on it. A section of newspaper folded into a boat that said, "Do you think clams get seasick?" And, of course, the bagel.

It bothered Nikki that Renee was still funny and still having fun while Nikki felt lost. Leah had drifted away as though Renee was all that had kept the three of them together and without Renee to laugh at her jokes, Nikki couldn't seem to be funny. She couldn't even tell if she was having fun.

Kim stood behind the counter of The Sweet Tooth candy store, a long string of red licorice hanging from her mouth. She looked up when Nikki came in. "You're late."

"So?" Nikki asked.

"Boss's son's in the back," Kim said.

Kim loved anime so passionately that she convinced their boss to stock Pocky and lychee gummies and green tea and ginger candies with hard surfaces but runny, spicy insides. They'd done so well that the Boss started asking Kim's opinion on all the new orders. She acted like he'd made her manager.

Nikki liked all the candy—peanut butter taffy, lime green foil-wrapped "alien coins" with chocolate discs inside, gummy geckos and gummy sidewinders and a whole assortment of translucent gummy fruit, long strips of paper dotted with sugar dots, shining and jagged rock candy, hot-as-Hell atomic fireballs, sticks of violet candy that tasted like flowery chalk, giant multi-colored spiral lollipops, not to mention chocolate-covered malt balls, chocolate-covered blueberries and raspberries and peanuts, and even tiny packages of chocolate-covered ants.

The pay was pretty much crap, but Nikki was allowed to eat as much candy as she wanted. She picked out a coffee toffee to start with because it seemed breakfast-y.

The boss's son came out of the stock room, his sleeveless t-shirt thin enough that Nikki could see the hair that covered his back and chest through the cloth. He scowled at her. "Most girls get sick of the candy after a while," he said, in a tone that was half grudging admiration, half panic at the profits vanishing through her teeth.

Nikki paused in her consumption of a pile of sour gummy lizards, their hides crunchy with granules of sugar. "Sorry," she said.

That seemed to be the right answer, because he turned to Kim and told her to restock the pomegranate jellybeans.

Nikki's stomach growled and, while his back was turned, she popped another lizard into her mouth.

The glass-enclosed waiting area of the bus stop was full when Nikki finished her shift. Rain slicked her skin and plastered her hair to her face and neck. By the time the bus came, she was soaked and even more convinced that her summer was doomed.

Nikki pushed her way into one of the few remaining seats, next to an old guy who smelled like a sulfurous fart. It took her a moment to realize he was the houndstooth suit-and-cane guy from the bus stop that morning. He'd probably been riding the bus this whole time. Still jittery from sugar, she could feel the headache-y start of a post-candy crash in her immediate future. Nikki tried to ignore the heavy wetness of her clothes and to breathe as shallowly as possible to avoid the old guy's stink.

The bus lurched forward. A woman chatting on her cell phone stumbled into Nikki's knee.

"'Scuse me," the woman said sharply, as though Nikki was the one who fell.

"I'm going to give you what you want," the man next to her whispered. Weirdly, his breath was like honey.

Nikki didn't reply. Nice breath or not, he was still a stinky, senile old pervert.

"I'm talking to you, girl." He touched her arm.

She turned toward him. "You're not supposed to talk to people on buses."

His cheeks wrinkled up as he smiled. "Is that so?"

"Yeah, trains too. It's a mass-transportation thing. Anything stuffed with people, you're supposed to act like you're alone."

"Is that what you want?" he asked. "You want everyone to act like you're not here?"

"Pretty much. You going to give me what I want?" Nikki asked, hoping he would shut up. She wished she could just tell freakjobs to fuck off, but she hated that hurt look that they sometimes got. It made her think of Boo. She would put up with a lot to not see that look.

He nodded. "I sure am."

The 'scuse-me woman looked in their direction, blinked, then plopped her fat ass right on Nikki's lap. Nikki yelped and the woman got up, red-faced.

"What are you doing there?" the 'scuse-me lady gasped.

The old pervert started laughing so hard that spit flew out of his mouth.

"Sitting," Nikki said. "What the hell are you doing?"

The woman turned away from Nikki, muttering to herself.

"You're very fortunate to be sitting next to me," the pervert said.

"How do you figure that?"

He laughed again, hard and long. "I gave you what you wanted.

I'll give you the next thing you want, too." He winked a rheumy eye. "For a price."

"Whatever," Nikki muttered.

"You know where to find me."

Mercifully, the next stop was Nikki's. She shoved the 'scuse-me woman hard as she pushed her way off the bus.

The rain had let up. Doug sat on the steps of the trailer, his hair frizzy with drizzle. He looked grim.

"What's going on?" Nikki asked. "Only managed to eat half your body weight?

"Boo's been hit," he said, voice rough. "Trevor hit your dog."

For a moment, Nikki couldn't breathe. The world seemed to speed up around her, cars streaking along the highway, the wind tossing wet leaves across the lot.

She thought about the raven tattoo on Trevor's back and wished someone would rip it off along with his skin. She wanted to tear him into a thousand pieces.

She thought about the old pervert on the bus.

I'll give you the next thing you want, too.

You know where to find me.

"Where's Boo now?" Nikki asked.

"At the vet. Mom wanted me to drive you over as soon as you got home."

"Why was he outside? Who let him out?"

"Mom came home with groceries. He slipped past her."

"Is he oka—?"

Doug shook his head. "They're waiting for you before they put him down. They wanted to give you a chance to say goodbye."

She wanted to throw up or scream or cry, but when she spoke, her voice sounded so calm that it unnerved her. "Why? Isn't there anything they can do?"

"Listen, the doctor said they could operate, but it's a couple thousand dollars and you know we can't afford it." Doug's voice was soft, like he was sorry, but she wanted to hit him anyway.

Nikki looked across the lot, but the truck wasn't in front of Trevor's trailer and his windows were dark. "We could make Trevor pay."

Doug sighed. "Not going to happen."

Now she felt tears well in her eyes, but she blinked them back. She wouldn't grieve over Boo. She'd save him. "I'm not going anywhere with you."

"You have to, Nikki. Mom's waiting for you."

"Call her. Tell her I'll be there in an hour. I'm taking the bus." Nikki grabbed the sleeve of Doug's jacket, gripping it as hard as she could. "She better not do anything to Boo until I get there." Tears slid down her cheek. She ignored them, concentrating on looking as fierce as possible. "You better not, either."

"Calm down. I'm not going to—" Doug said, but she was already walking away.

Nikki got on the next bus that stopped and scanned the aisles for the old pervert. A woman with two bags of groceries cradled on her lap looked up at Nikki, then abruptly turned away. A man stretched out on the long back seat shifted in his sleep, his fingers curled tightly around a bottle of beer. Three men in green coveralls conversed softly. There was no one else.

Nikki slid into her seat, wrapping her arms around her body as though she could hold in her sobs with sheer pressure. She had no idea what to do. Looking for a weird old guy who could grant wishes was pathetic. It was sad and stupid.

If there was some way to get the money, things might be different. She thought of all the stuff in the trailer that could be sold, but it didn't add up to a thousand dollars. Even sticking her hand into the till at The Sweet Tooth was unlikely to net more than a few hundred.

Outside the window, the strip malls and motels slid together in her tear-blurred vision. Nikki thought of the day she'd found Boo by the side of the road, dehydrated and bloody. With all those bite marks, she figured his owners had been fighting him against other dogs, but when he saw her he bounded up as dumb and sweet and trusting as if he'd been pampered since he was a puppy. If he died, nothing would ever be fair again.

The bus stopped in front of a churchyard, the doors opened, and the old guy got on. He wore a suit of shiny sharkskin and carried a cane with a silver greyhound instead of a knob. He still stank of rotten eggs, though. Worse than ever.

Nikki sat up straight, wiping her face with her sleeve. "Hey."

He looked over at her as though he didn't know her. "Excuse me?"

"I've been looking for you. I need your help."

Sitting down in the seat across the aisle, he unbuttoned the bottom button on his jacket. "That's magic to my ears."

"My dog." Nikki sank her fingernails into the flesh of her palm to keep herself calm. "Someone hit my dog and he's going to die . . ."

His face broke into a wrinkled grin. "And you want him to live. Like I've never heard that one before."

He was making fun of her, but she forced a smile. "So you'll do it."

He shook his head. "Nope."

"What do you mean? Why not?"

A long sigh escaped his lips, like he was already tired of the conversation. "Let's just say that it's not in my nature."

"What is that supposed to mean?"

He shifted the cane in his lap and she noticed that what she had thought of as a greyhound appeared to have three silver heads. He scowled at her, like a teacher when you missed an obvious answer and he knew you hadn't done the reading. "You have to give me something to get something."

"I've got forty bucks," she said, biting her lip. "I don't want to do any sex stuff."

"I am not entirely without sympathy." He shrugged his thin shoulders. "How about this—I will wager my services against something of yours. If you can beat me at any contest of your choosing, your dog will be well and you'll owe me nothing."

"Really? Any contest?" she asked.

He held out his hand. "Shake on it and we've got a deal."

His skin was warm and dry in her grip.

"So, what it going to be?" he asked. "You play the fiddle? Or maybe you'd like to try your hand at jump rope?"

She took a long look at him. He was slender and his clothes hung on him a bit, as though he'd been bigger when he'd bought them. He didn't look like a big eater. "An eating contest," she said. "I'm wagering that I can eat more than you can."

He laughed so hard she thought for a moment he was having a seizure. "That's a new one. Fine. I'm all appetite."

His reaction made her nervous. "Wait—" she said. "You never told me what you wanted if I lost."

"Just a little thing. You won't miss it." He indicated the door of the bus with his cane. "Next stop is yours. I'll be by tomorrow. Don't worry about your dog for tonight."

She stood. "First tell me what I'm going to lose."

"You'll overreact," he said, shaking his head.

"I won't," Nikki said, but she wasn't sure what she would do. What could he want? She'd said "no sex," but he hadn't made any promises.

The old guy held out his hands in a conciliatory gesture. "Your soul."

"What? Why would you want that?"

"I'm a collector. I have to have the whole set—complete. All souls. They're going to look *spectacular* all lined up. There was a time when I was close, but then there were all these special releases and I got behind. And forget about having them mint-in-box. I have to settle for what I can get these days."

"You're joking."

"Maybe." He looked out the window, as if considering all

those missing souls. "Don't worry. It's like an appendix. You won't even miss it."

Nikki walked home from the bus stop, her stomach churned as she thought over the bargain she'd made. Her soul. The devil. She had just made a bargain with the devil. Who else wanted to buy souls?

She stomped into the trailer to see her mom on the couch, eating a piece of frozen pizza. Doug sat next to her, watching a car being rebuilt on television. Both of them looked tired.

"Oh, honey," her mother said. "I'm so sorry."

Nikki sat down on the shag rug. "You didn't kill Boo, did you?"

"The vet said that we could wait until tomorrow and see how he's doing, but he wasn't very encouraging." Long fingers stroked Nikki's hair, but she refused to be soothed. "You have to think what would be best for the poor dog. You don't want him to suffer."

Nikki jumped up and stalked over to the kitchen. "I don't want him to die!"

"Go talk to your sister," their mother said. Doug pushed himself up off the couch.

"Show me how to train for an eating contest," Nikki told him, when he tried to speak. "Show me right now."

He shook his head. "You're seriously losing it."

"Yeah," she said. "But I need to win."

The next morning, after her mother left for work, Nikki called herself out sick and started straightening up the place. After all, the devil was the most famous guest she'd ever had. She'd heard of him, and, what was more, she was pretty sure he knew a lot of people she'd be impressed by.

He knocked on the door of the trailer around noon. Today, he wore a red double-breasted suit with a black shirt and tie. He carried a gnarled cane in a glossy brown, like polished walnut.

Seeing her looking at it, he smiled. "Bull penis. Not too many of these."

"You dress like a pimp," Nikki said before she thought better of it.

His smile just broadened.

"So are you *a* devil or *the* devil?" Nikki held the screen door open for him.

"I'm a devil to some." He winked as he walked past her. "But I'm the devil to you."

She shuddered. Suddenly, the idea of him being supernatural seemed entirely too real. "My brother's in the back waiting for us."

Nikki had set up on the picnic table in the common area of the trailer park. She walked onto the hot concrete and the devil followed her. Doug looked up from where he carefully counted out portions of sour gummy frogs onto paper plates. He looked like a giant, holding each tiny candy between two thick fingers.

Nikki brushed an earwig and some sour-cherry splatter off a bench and sat down. "Doug's going to explain the rules."

The devil sat down across from her and leaned his cane against the table. "Good. I'm starving."

Doug stood up, wiping sweaty palms on his jeans. "This is what we're going to do. We have a bag of one hundred and sixty-six sour gummy frogs. That's all we could get. I divided them into sixteen plates of ten and two plates of three, so you each have a maximum of eighty-three frogs. If you both eat the same number of frogs, whoever finishes their frogs first wins. If you have a . . . er . . . reversal of fortune, then you lose, period."

"He means if you puke," Nikki said.

Doug gave her a stern look but didn't say anything.

"We need not be limited by your supply," said the devil. A huge tarnished silver platter appeared on the table. It scuttled over to Nikki on chicken feet and she saw that it was heaped with sugar-studded frogs.

The candy on the paper plates looked dull in comparison with what glimmered on the table. Nikki picked up an orange-and-black-colored candy poison-dart frog and put it regretfully down. It just seemed dumb to let the devil supply food. "You have to use ours."

The devil shrugged. With a wave of his hand, the dish of frogs disappeared, leaving nothing behind but a burnt-sugar smell. "Very well."

Doug put a plastic pitcher of water and two glasses between them. "Okay," he said, lifting up a stopwatch. "Go!"

Nikki started eating. The salty sweet flavor flooded her mouth as she crammed in candy.

Across the table, the devil lifted up his first paper plate, rolling it up and using the tube to pour frogs into a mouth that seemed to expand. His jaw unhinged like a snake. He picked up a second plate.

Nikki swallowed frog after frog, sugar scraping her throat, racing to catch up.

Doug slid a new pile in front of Nikki and she started eating. She was in the zone. One frog, then another, then a sip of water. The cloying sweetness scraped her throat raw, but she kept eating.

The devil poured a third plate of candy down his throat, then a fourth. At the seventh plate, the devil paused with a groan. He untucked his shirt and undid the button on his dress pants to pat his engorged belly. He looked full.

Nikki stuffed candy in her mouth, suddenly filled with hope.

The devil chuckled and unsheathed a knife from the top of his cane.

"What are you doing?" Doug shouted.

"Just making room," the devil said. Pressing the blade to his belly, he slit a line in his stomach. Dozens upon dozens of gooey half-chewed frogs tumbled into the dirt.

Nikki stared at him, paralyzed with dread. Her fingers still held a frog, but she didn't bring it to her lips. She had no hope of winning.

Doug looked away from the mess of partially digested candy. "That's cheating!"

The devil tipped up the seventh plate into his widening mouth and swallowed ten frogs at once. "Nothing in the rules against it."

Nikki wondered what it would be like have no soul. Would she barely miss it? Could she still dream? Without one, would she have no more guilt or fear or fun? Maybe without a soul she wouldn't even care that Boo was dead.

The devil cheated. If she wanted to win, she had to cheat, too.

On her sixth plate, Nikki started sweating, but she knew she could finish. She just couldn't finish before he did.

She had to beat him in quantity. She had to eat more sour gummy frogs than he did.

"I feel sick," Nikki said.

"Don't *you know.*" Doug shook his head vigorously. "Fight it."

Nikki bent over, holding her stomach. While hidden by the table, she picked up one of the slimy, chewed up frogs that had been in the devil's stomach and popped it in her mouth. The frog tasted like sweetness and dirt and something rotten.

The nausea was real this time. She choked and forced herself to swallow around the sour taste of her own gorge.

Sitting up, she saw that the devil had finished all his frogs. She still had two more plates to go.

"I win," the devil said. "No need to keep eating."

Doug sunk fingers into his hair and tugged. "He's right."

"No way." Nikki gulped down another mouthful of candy. "I'm finishing my plates."

She ate and ate, ignoring how the rubbery frogs stuck in her throat. She kept eating. Swallowed the last sour-gummy frog, she stood up. "Are you finished?"

"I've been finished for ages," said the devil.

"Then *I* win."

The devil yawned. "Impossible."

"I ate one more frog than you did," she said. "So I win."

He pointed his cane at Doug. "If you cheated and gave her another frog, we'll be doing this contest over and you'll be joining us."

Doug shook his head. "It took me an hour to count out

those frogs. They were exactly even."

"I ate one of the frogs from your gut," Nikki said. "I picked it up off the ground and I ate it."

"That's disgusting!" Doug said.

"Five-second rule," Nikki said. "If it's in the devil for less than five seconds, it's still good."

"That's *cheating,*" said the devil. He sounded half-admiring and half-appalled, reminding her of her boss's son at The Sweet Tooth.

She shook her head. "Nothing in the rules against it."

The devil scowled for a moment, then bowed shallowly. "Well done, Nicole. Count on seeing me again soon." With those words, he ambled toward the bus station. He paused in front of Trevor's trailer, pulled out a handful of envelopes from the mailbox, and kept going.

Nikki's mother's car pulled into the lot, Boo's head visible in the passenger-side window. His tongue lolled despite the absurd cone-shaped collar around his neck.

Nikki hopped up on top of the picnic table and shrieked with joy, leaping around, the sugar and adrenaline and relief making her giddy.

She stopped jumping. "You know what?"

Doug looked up at her. "What?"

"I think my summer is starting not to suck so much."

He sat down on a bench so hard that she heard the wood strain. The look he gave her was pure disbelief.

"So," Nikki asked, "you want to get some lunch?"

The Boy Who Cried Wolf

THERE'S A CERTAIN KIND of boy who likes to read only about things that have really happened. Like Alex. He read about the *Titanic* and memorized how many people died (1,523) and the name of the boat that picked up the survivors (*RMS Carpathia*). He read about ghosts and werewolves, too, sometimes, but only when he was certain he was being presented with facts. (The vulnerability to silver bullets, for example, was made up by modern fiction writers—probably any bullet would do.)

In one of the books Alex took out of the library, there was a story about a white flower, the scent of which turned people into wolves. He worried about the flower. It seemed to have no proper name for him to memorize.

In the summers, Alex's parents took he and his younger sister, Anna, sailing. For two weeks, they slept on scratchy cushions in a tiny room in the prow of the boat. Alex mostly sat on deck, his skin tightening with sunburn even though it was slathered with coconut-smelling lotion and his hair stiffening with salt as he read. Sometimes the glow of the sun on the paper was almost blinding.

Anna swung around one of the fasts. She'd been running around the deck all day in a red bathing suit and a floppy hat, dancing up to him and trying to get him to play games with her. Meanwhile, Dad fished off the back and Mom steered lazily. There was barely any wind and the swells were small. Alex was bored but comfortable.

"Want a plum?" Mom called, reaching into a cooler.

"Nah," Dad said. "Alex just wants to sit there with his nose in a book. All this beautiful nature around and he doesn't want to experience any of it."

Alex ducked under the mast and took the fruit, frowning at his dad. He bit into it as he resettled into the cockpit. The plum was mealy and less sweet than he thought it would be. The juice ran over his hand.

The book on Alex's lap was about sharks. He imagined them, darting beneath the boat, sleek and hungry. Mako sharks were the fastest—but pelagic, meaning they liked deep water. They seldom surfaced. According to what he had read, the great white shark could swim anywhere. In any kind of water. He kept his eyes on the water, looking for thin, angular fins.

Sharks would eat anything. He considered dropping his plum over the side. He bet that so long as it was moving, a shark would eat it. It was the movement that enticed them.

If one did come, then Alex would tell them what to do. Alex would be a hero. Even his dad would think so.

"Mom," Anna said. "When can we swim?"

"When we anchor," Mom said.

"When will we anchor?" Anna asked, the whine in her voice more pronounced.

"Depends on the wind," Dad said. "But it won't be more than a hour."

"You said that an hour ago," said Alex, but he didn't mind. He liked reading about sharks with all that deep water underneath him.

In a little more than two hours, they anchored off a lagoon in Jamaica. They'd flown into Montego Bay a week ago and had been working their way down the coast. Most nights they inflated the dinghy and rowed in for ginger beer and dinner at one of the little fish places along the shore. Tonight, though, there was no town, just a lagoon and Mom, boiling potatoes in the galley.

The beach was nice. No coral to cut up their feet. Anna paddled near some rocks, picking up snails and trying to catch the little lizards that seemed to be everywhere. She chased one into the water and then scooped it up, triumphant.

Alex walked on the beach, looking for shells. Dad scooped sand out of a hole, ready to start a fire and grill the grouper he'd bought the day before. Mom's potatoes finished boiling and she brought them over, wrapped in tin foil, to stick in the fire.

That was when Alex spotted them. The white flowers.

They grew among the scrub, near a banana tree crawling with ants. Tiny buds of white on long stalks. Like the pen-and-ink illustration in the compendium about werewolves. He wasn't sure, but what if they were the *same kind*?

In the story, two children had been out picking flowers when they stumbled upon the white ones. After gathering a few stems, they turned into wolves and raced home to eat their parents.

What if Anna picked one? Alex imagined her sprouting fur and how upset his parents would be, how convinced that she would never hurt them. When she went for Dad's neck, Mom would still be sure that Anna was only attacking because she was scared.

But what if Mom or Dad were the ones that picked a flower?

He'd have to run for the flowers, smell them fast and hope that he turned into a wolf too. But it was too easy to imagine if fast wasn't fast enough. He thought of sharks.

"Hungry?" Dad called to him.

His stomach rumbled in answer and he felt sick.

What if the scent could blow to them? What if they didn't even need to get close to the flowers?

He wanted to tell his parents about werewolves and have them row back out to the boat, but that plan would never work. Dad didn't believe the facts that Alex read if they contradicted his ideas about things. *Just because it's in a book,* he was fond of saying, *that doesn't make it true.*

Alex could just imagine his father sniffing the flower to prove his point.

Anna ran up to where Dad was cooking the grouper. Her legs were covered in sand and she had on a hooded cover-up over her bathing suit. "Is it almost done?" she asked.

The fire lit her eyes. As he looked at his father and mother, he saw the flames reflect in their eyes too. He shuddered.

What if he went and sniffed the flower first? Then *he* would be the wolf. Then he would have no reason to be afraid. And if he started turning, he could tell them to run and get off the island before he finished transforming. He would know what was happening. He would be *experiencing* nature.

And if the flowers weren't the flowers from the book, no one would know he'd made a mistake or that he'd been so worried about his own family eating him up.

He took a step toward the flowers. Then another. He imagined the scent of them drifting to him, a combination of his mother's perfume and sweat. That couldn't be the real smell.

"Alex," Mom called. "The food's done. What are you looking for?"

"Is there a lizard?" Anna asked. She was heading toward him.

"No," he said. "I just have to pee." That stopped Anna.

The white flowers blew in the breeze. His heart was beating so hard that he felt like he couldn't catch his breath, like each beat was a punch in the chest. He reached for a bud, pulling it free. The plant sprang back, petals scattering. He brought the single flower to his nose, crushing it, inhaling sharply.

He was hungry, hungrier than he could remember being in a long while. He thought of the plum and tried to remember why he hadn't finished it.

"Wash your hands in the ocean when you're done," his mother said. Alex was so surprised by her voice that he dropped the blossom. She didn't know what he was doing, he reminded himself.

Ripping the plant out of the ground, he shredded it. Just to be safe. Just to be sure.

He walked back to the fire, waiting for his skin to start itching. It didn't.

Alex ate two potatoes, three ears of corn, and most of the tail of the fish. He felt good, so full of relief that when Anna bounced up to him in the light of the setting sun and wanted to play tic-tac-toe in the wet sand, he agreed.

She drew the board in the sand and made a big X in the middle. "Okay," she said. "Your turn."

He drew an O in the upper left-hand corner. Their mother was gathering up the plates to take back to the boat. He wondered if she was going to make dessert. He was still kind of hungry.

Anna drew an X in the bottom right corner. He hated going second. One of the facts of tic-tac-toe was that the person who goes first is twice as likely to win as the person who goes second.

Looking at Anna's red bathing suit through the hooded cover-up made it seem like he could see past her skin to the raw meat underneath. His stomach growled and Anna laughed. She found every gross body sound to be hysterical.

"Come on, kids," their mother called. "It's too dark to play."

He looked up. There was only a sliver of a moon. The sun had slid all the way under the water.

Alex's stomach cramped and he winced. He thought about the fish, sitting in the ice chest all day. Maybe it had gone bad.

Anna laughed. "You should see your face. Your eyes got really big. Big enough to—"

His hands cramped, too, curling up into claws. Anna stopped laughing.

"Mom!" he yelled, panicked. His vision shifted, went blurry. "Mom!"

Anna shrieked.

"What's the matter?" His mother's voice sounded close and he remembered that he was supposed to warn them.

"Get away!" His voice broke on the last word as another wave of pain hit him. "Stay away from the flowers!" That made no sense. How was she supposed to understand that?

He opened his mouth to explain when his bones wrenched themselves sideways. He could hear them pop out of sockets. His scream became a howl. Fur split his skin.

New smells washed over him. Fear. Food. Fire.

Anna came into focus, racing across the beach toward their father. He could feel his ears lift, his mouth water. He leapt up onto all fours.

Sharks were right. It was the movement that was enticing.

"*Alex,*" his mother said, bending down, reaching toward him. As if he would never hurt her. His gaze went to her throat.

"Laura!" his father shouted. "Get away from that animal! Where's Alex?"

Alex opened his mouth to answer, but the words came out a growl, low and terrible. The quick flash of terror in his father's face made him salivate. He had to run. Before. Before. Before something happened. Banana leaves brushed his back, and he nearly tripped over long banyan roots. He kept moving, his nose full of rich scents. Lizards. Beetles. Soil. Salt. He was so very hungry.

Just keep running, he told himself. Like a shark through deep water.

Alex tried to think of all the things he knew about wolves. They could travel long distances. They hunted in packs and howled to demonstrate territory, but barked when nervous.

His red tongue lolled as he panted.

None of those facts meant anything anymore.

He came to a house in the woods with a roof of corrugated metal. An old woman with salt-and-pepper hair hung brightly colored sheets on a line. She sang as she worked. A basket sat beside her, full of laundry. She looked so kind, like someone's mother, someone's grandmother. His mouth watered and he crept closer.

She might be someone's grandmother, but at least she wasn't his.

THE NIGHT MARKET

TOMASA WALKED DOWN THE road, balancing the basket of offerings on her head. Her mother would have been angry to see her carrying things like one of the maids. Even though it was night and there had been a heavy rain that day, the road was hot under Tomasa's sandaled feet. She tried to focus on the heat and not on the bottle of strong *lambanog* clinking against the dish of *paksiw na pata* or the smell of the rice cakes steamed in coconut. It would be very bad luck to eat the *parangál* that was supposed to bribe an elf into lifting his curse.

Not that she'd ever seen an elf. She wasn't even sure if she believed the story that her sister, Eva, had told when she'd rushed in, clutching broken pieces of tamarind pod, hair streaming with water. Usually, the sisters walked home from school together. But today, when it started to rain, Eva had ducked under a tree and declared that she would wait out the storm. Tomasa had thought nothing of it—Eva hated to be dirty or wet or windblown.

She kicked a shard of coconut shell out into the road, scattering red ants. She shouldn't have left Eva. It all came down to that. Even though Eva was older, she had no sense. Especially around boys.

A car slowed as it passed. Tomasa kept her eyes on the road and after a moment it sped away. Girls didn't usually go walking the streets of Alaminos alone at night. The Philippines just wasn't safe—people got kidnapped or killed, even this far outside Manila. But with her father and the driver out in the provinces and her mother in Hong Kong for the week, there was only Tomasa and their maid, Rosa, left to decide who would bring the gift. Eva was too sick to do much of anything. Rosa said that was what happened when an *enkanto* fell in love—his beloved would sicken just as his heart sickened with desire.

Looking at Eva's pale face, Tomasa had said she would go. After all, no elf would fall in love with her. She touched her right cheek. She could trace the shape of her birthmark without even looking in a mirror—an irregular splash of red that covered one of her eyes and stopped just above her lips.

Tomasa kept walking, past the whitewashed church, the narrow line of shops at the edge of town, and the city's single McDonald's. Then the buildings began to thin. Spanish-style houses flanked the road, while rice fields spread out beyond them into the distance. Mosquitoes buzzed close, drawn by her sweat.

By the time Tomasa crossed the short bridge near her school, only the light of the moon let her see where to put her feet. She stepped carefully through thick plants and hopped over a ditch. The tamarind tree was unremarkable—a wide trunk clouded by thick, feathery leaves. She set her basket down among the roots.

At least the moon was only half-full. On full-moon nights, Rosa said that witches and elves and other spirits met at a market in the graveyard where they traded things like people did during the day. Not that she thought it was true, but it was still frightening.

"*Tabi-tabi po*," she whispered to the darkness, just like Rosa had told her, warning him that she was there. "Please take these offerings and let my sister get better."

There was only silence and Tomasa felt even more foolish than before. She turned to go.

Something rustled in the branches above her.

Tomasa froze and the sound stopped. She wanted to believe it was the wind, but the night air was warm and stagnant.

She looked up into eyes the green of unripe bananas.

"Hello," she stammered, heart thundering in her chest.

The *enkanto* stepped out onto one of the large limbs of the tree. His skin was the same dark cinnamon as a tamarind pod and his feet were bare. His clothes surprised her—cutoff jeans and a t-shirt with a cracked and faded logo on it. He might have been a boy from the rice fields if it wasn't for his too-bright eyes and the fact that the branch hadn't so much as dipped under his weight.

He smiled down at her and she could not help but notice that he was beautiful. "What if I don't make your sister well?" he asked.

Tomasa didn't know what to say. She had lost track of the conversation. She was still trying to decide if she was willing to believe in elves. "What?"

He jumped down from his perch and she took a quick step away from him.

The elf boy picked up the *lambanog* and twisted the cap free. His hair rustled like leaves. "The food—is it freely given?"

"I don't understand."

"Is it mine whether I make your sister better or not?"

She forced herself to concentrate on his question. Both answers seemed wrong. If she said that the food was payment, it wasn't a gift, was it? And if it wasn't a gift, then she wasn't really following Rosa's directions. "I suppose so," she said finally.

"Ah, good," the elf said and took a deep swallow of the liquor. His smile said that she'd given the wrong answer. She felt cold, despite the heat.

"You're not going to make her better," she said.

That only made his smile widen. "Let me give you something else in return—something better." He reached up into the foliage and snapped off a brown tamarind pod. Bringing it to his lips, he whispered a few words and then kissed it. "Whoever eats this will love you."

Tomasa's face flushed. "I don't want anyone to love me." She didn't need an elf to tell her that she was ugly. "I want my sister not to be sick."

"Take it," he said, putting the tamarind in her hand and closing her fingers over it. He tilted his head. "It is all you'll get from me tonight."

The elf was standing very close to her now, her hand clasped in both of his. His skin felt dry and slightly rough in a way that made her think of bark. Somehow, she had gotten tangled up in her thoughts and was no longer sure of what she ought to say.

He raised his eyebrows thoughtfully. His too-bright eyes reflected the moonlight like an animal's. Tomasa was filled with a sudden, nameless fear.

"I have to go," she said, pulling her hand free.

Over the bridge and down the familiar streets, past the closed shops, her feet finding their way by habit, Tomasa ran home. Her panic was amplified with each step, until she was racing the dark. Only when she got close to home did she slow, her shirt soaked with sweat and her muscles hurting, the pod still clasped in her hand.

Rosa was waiting on the veranda of their house, smoking one of the clove cigarettes that her brother sent by the carton from Indonesia. She got up when Tomasa walked through the gate.

"Did you see him?" Rosa asked. "Did he take the offering?"

"Yes and yes," Tomasa said, breathing hard. "But it doesn't matter."

Rosa frowned. "You really saw an *enkanto*? You're sure."

Tomasa had been a coward. Perspiration cooling on her neck, she thought of all the things she might have said. He'd caught her off guard. She hadn't expected him to have a soft smile, or to laugh, or even to exist in the first place. She looked at the tamarind shell in her hand and watched as her fingers crushed it. Bits of the pod stuck in the sticky brown fruit beneath. For all that she'd thought Eva was stupid around boys, she'd been the stupid one. "I'm sure," she said hollowly.

On her way up the stairs to bed, it occurred to Tomasa to wonder for the first time why an elf who could make a love spell with a few words would burn with thwarted desire. But then, in all of Rosa's stories the elves were wicked and strange—beings that cursed and blessed according to their whims. Maybe there was just no making sense of it.

The next day the priest came and said novenas. And after that, the *albularyo* sprinkled the white sheets of Eva's bed with herbs. Then the doctor came and gave her some pills. But by nightfall, Eva was no better. Her skin, which had been as brown as polished mahogany, was pale and dusty as that of a snake ready to shed.

Tomasa called her father's cell phone and left a message, but she wasn't sure if he would get it. Out far enough in the provinces, getting a signal was chancy at best. Her mother's Hong Kong hotel was easier to reach. She left another message and went up to see her sister.

Eva's hair was damp with sweat and her eyes were fever-bright when Tomasa came to sit at the end of her bed. Candles and crucifixes littered the side table, along with a pot of strong and smelly herb tea.

Eva grabbed Tomasa's hand and clutched it hard enough to hurt.

"I heard what you did." Eva said with a cough. "Stay away from his goddamned tree."

Tomasa grinned. "You should drink more of the tea. It's supposed to help."

Eva grimaced and made no move toward her cup. Maybe it tasted as bad as it smelled. "Look, I'm serious," she said.

"Tell me again how he cursed you," Tomasa said. "I'm serious, too."

Eva gave a weird little laugh. "I should have listened to Rosa's stories. Maybe if I'd read a couple less magazines . . . I don't know. I just thought he was a boy from the fields. I told him to mind his place and leave me alone."

"You didn't eat any of his fruit, right?" Tomasa asked suddenly.

"I had a little piece," Eva said, looking at the wall. "Before I knew he was there."

That was bad. Tomasa took a deep breath and tried to think of how to phrase her next question. "Do you . . . um . . . do you think he might have made you fall in love with him?"

"Are you crazy?" Eva blew her nose in a tissue. "Love him? Like him? He's not even human."

Tomasa forced herself to smile, but in her heart, she worried.

Rosa was sitting at a plastic table in the kitchen chunking up cubes of ginger while garlicky chicken simmered on the stove. Tomasa liked the kitchen. Unlike the rest of the house, it was small and dark. The floor was poured concrete instead of gleaming wood. A few herbs grew in rusted coffee cans along the windowsill and there was a strong odor of sugarcane vinegar. It was a kitchen to be useful in.

Tomasa sat down on a stool. "Tell me about elves."

Rosa looked up from her chopping, a cigarette dangling from her lips. She breathed smoke from her nose. "What do you want me to tell you?"

"Anything. Everything. Something that might help."

"They're fickle as cats and twice as cruel. You know the tales. They'll steal your heart if you let them and if you don't, they'll curse you for your good sense. They're night things—spirits—and don't care for the day. They don't like gold, either. It reminds them of the sun."

"I know all that," Tomasa said. "Tell me something I don't know."

Rosa shook her head. "I'm no *mananambal*—I only know the stories. His love will fade; he will forget your sister and she will get well again."

Tomasa pressed her lips into a thin line. "What if she doesn't?"

"It has only been two days. Be patient. Not even a cold would go away in that time."

Two days turned into three and then four. Their mother had changed her flight and was due home that Tuesday, but there was still no word from their father. By Sunday, Tomasa found that she couldn't wait anymore. She went to the shed and got a machete. She put her gold Santa Maria pendant on a chain and fastened it around her neck. Steeling herself, she walked to the tamarind tree, although her legs felt like lead and her stomach churned.

In the day, the tree looked frighteningly normal. Leafy green, sun-dappled, and buzzing with flies.

She hefted the machete. "Make Eva well."

The leaves rustled with the wind, but no elf appeared.

She swung the knife at the trunk of the tree. It stuck in the wood, knocking off a piece of bark, but her hand slid forward on the blade and the sharp steel slit open her palm. She let go of the machete and watched the shallow cut well with blood.

"You'll have to do better than that," she said, wiping her hand against her jeans. She worked the blade free from the trunk and hefted it to swing again.

But somehow her grip must have been loose, because the machete tumbled from her hands before she could complete the arc. It flew off into the brush by the stream.

Tomasa stomped off in the direction of where it had fallen, but she found no trace of it in the thick weeds. "Fine," she shouted at the tree. "Fine!"

"Aren't you afraid of me?" a voice said, and Eva whirled around. The elf was standing in the grass with the machete in his hand.

She found herself speechless again. If anything the daylight rendered him more alien looking. His eyes glittered and his hair seemed to move with a subtle wind as though he was underwater.

He took a step toward her, his feet keeping to the shadows. "I've heard it's very bad luck to cut down an *enkanto's* tree."

Tomasa thought of the gold pendant around her neck and stepped into a patch of sunlight. "Good thing for me that it's only a little chipped, then."

He snorted and for a moment he looked like he was going to smile. "What if I told you that whatever you do to the tree, you do to the spirit?"

"You look fine," she said, edging back to the bridge. He did. She was the one who was bleeding.

"You're either brave or stupid." He turned the blade in his hand and held it out to her, hilt first. She would have to step closer to him, into the shadows, to take it.

"Well, I'd pick stupid," she said. "But not that stupid." She walked quickly over the bridge, leaving him still holding the machete.

Her heart beat like a drum in her chest as she made her way home.

That night, lying in bed, Tomasa heard distant music. When she turned toward the window, a full moon looked down on her. Quickly, she dressed in the dark, careful to clasp her gold chain around her neck. Holding her shoes in one hand, she crept down the stairs, bare feet making only a soft slap on the wood.

She would find a *mananambal* to remove the *enkanto's* curse. She would go to the night market herself.

The graveyard was at the edge of town, where the electrical lines stopped running. The moonlight illuminated the distant rice fields where kerosene lamps flickered in Nipa huts. Cicadas called from the trees and beneath her feet, thorny touch-me-nots curled up with each step.

Close to the cemetery, the Japanese synth-pop was loud enough to recognize and she saw lights. Two men with machine guns slung over their shoulders stood near marble steps. A generator chugged away near the trees, long black cords connecting it to floodlights mounted on tombs. All across the graves a market had been set up, collapsible tables covered with cloth and wares, and people squatting among the stones.

From this distance, they didn't look like elves or witches or anything supernatural at all. Still, she didn't want to be rude. Unclasping the Santa Maria pendant from her neck, she put it in her mouth. She tasted the salt of her sweat and tried to find a place for it between her cheek and her tongue.

She wondered if the men with guns would stop her, but they

let her pass without so much as a glance. A man on the edge of the tables played a little tune on a nose flute. He smiled at her and she tried to grin back, even though his teeth were unusually long and his smile seemed a touch too wide.

A few vendors squatting in front of baskets called to Tomasa as she passed. Piles of golden mangos and papaya paled in the moonlight. Foul-smelling durians hung from a line. The eggplant and purple yams looked black and strange, while a heap of ginger root resembled misshapen dolls.

At another table, split carcasses of goats were spread out like blankets. Inside a loose cage of bamboo, frogs hopped frantically. Nearby was a collection of eggs, some of which seemed too slender and leathery for chickens.

"What is that?" Tomasa asked.

"Snake *balut*," said the old woman behind the table. She spit red into the dirt and Tomasa told herself that the woman was only chewing betel nut. Lots of people chewed betel nut. There was nothing strange about it.

"Snake's tasty," the vendor went on. "Better than crow, but I have that, too."

Tomasa took two steps back from the table and then braced herself. She needed help and this woman was already speaking with her.

"I'm looking for a *mananambal* that can take an *enkanto's* spell off my sister," she said.

The old woman grinned, showing crimson-stained teeth and pointed past the largest building. "Look for the man selling potions."

Tomasa set off in that direction. Outside an open tomb,

men argued over prices in front of tables spread with guns. A woman with teeth as white as coconut meat smiled at Tomasa, one arm draped around a man, and her upper body hovering in the air. She had no lower body. Wet innards flashed from beneath a beaded shirt as she moved.

Tomasa rolled the golden pendant on her tongue, her hands shaking. No one else seemed to notice.

A line of women dressed in tight clothing leaned against the outside wall of the tomb. One had skin that was far too pale, while another had feet that were turned backwards. Some of them looked like girls Tomasa knew from town, but they stared blankly at her as she passed. Tomasa shuddered and kept moving.

She passed vendors selling horns and powders, narcotics and charms. There were candles rubbed with thick salves and small clay figurines wound with bits of hair. One man sat behind a table with several iron pots smoking over a small grill.

Steam rose from them, making the hot night hotter. Bunches of herbs and flowers littered the table, along with several empty Johnny Walker and Jim Beam bottles and a chipped, ceramic funnel.

The man looked up from ladling a solution into one of the empties. His longish hair was streaked with gray and when he smiled at her, she saw that one of his teeth had been replaced with gold.

"This one has a hundred herbs boiled in coconut oil," he said, pointing to one of the pots. "*Haplas,* will cure anything." He pointed to another. "And here, *gayuma,* for luck or love."

"*Lolo,*" she said with a slight bob of her head. "I need

something for my sister. An *enkanto* has fallen in love with her and she's sick."

"To break curses. *Sumpa,* an antidote." He indicated a third pot.

"How much?" Tomasa asked, reaching for her pockets.

His grin widened. "Wouldn't you like to assure yourself that I'm the real thing?"

Tomasa stopped, unsure of herself. What was the right answer?

"What's that in your mouth?" he asked.

"Just a pit. I bought a plum," she lied.

"You shouldn't eat the fruit here," he said, extending his hand. "Here. Spit it out. Let me see."

Tomasa shook her head.

"Come on." He smiled. "If you don't trust me a little, how can you trust me to cure your sister?"

Tomasa hesitated, but she thought of Eva, flushed and pale. She spat the golden pendant into his palm.

He cackled, the sound dry in his throat. "You're more clever than I thought."

She didn't know if she should be pleased or not.

One of the *mananambal's* fingers darted out to dot her forehead with oil. She felt wobbly.

"What did you do?" she managed to ask. Her voice sounded thick and slow as smoke.

"You're a fine piece of flesh, even with that face. I'll get more than I could use in a thousand brews."

It sounded like nonsense to Tomasa. Her head had started to spin and all she wanted to do was sit down in the dirt and rest.

But the gold-toothed man had her by the arm and was dragging her away from his table.

She stumbled along, knocking into a man in a wide straw hat who was running down the aisle of vendors. When he caught hold of her, she saw that his eyes were green as grass.

"You," she said, her voice syrup-slow. She stumbled and fell on her hands and knees. People were shouting at each other, but that wasn't so bad because at least no one was making her get up. Her necklace had fallen in the dirt beside her. She forced herself to close her hand over it.

The elf pushed the *mananambal,* saying something that she couldn't quite understand because all the words seemed to slur together. The old man shoved back and then, grabbing the *enkanto*'s arm at the wrist, bit down with his golden tooth.

The elf gasped in pain and brought down his fist on the old man's head, knocking him backwards. The bitten arm hung limply from the elf's side.

Tomasa struggled to her feet, fighting off the thickness that threatened to overwhelm her. Something was wrong. The potion vender had done this to her. She narrowed her eyes at him.

The *mananambal* grinned, his tooth glinting in the floodlights.

"Come on," he said, reaching for her.

"Leave me alone," she managed to say, stumbling back. The *enkanto* caught her before she fell, supporting her with his good arm.

"Let her alone," said the *enkanto,* "or I will curse you blind, lame, and worse."

The old man laughed. "I'm a curse breaker, fool."

The elf grabbed one of the Jim Beam bottles from the table and slammed it down, so that he was holding a jagged glass neck. The elf smiled a very thin smile. "Then I won't bother with magic."

The old man went silent. Together, Tomasa and the elf stumbled out of the night market. Once the music had faded into the distance, they sank down beneath a balete tree.

"Why?" she asked, still a little light-headed.

He looked down and hesitated before he answered. "You're brave to go to the night market alone." He made a little laugh. "If something had happened to you, it would have been my fault."

"I thought I was just stupid," she said. She felt stupid. "Please, end this, let my sister get better."

"No," he said suddenly, standing up.

"If you really loved her, you would let her get better," said Tomasa.

"But I don't love her," the *enkanto* said.

Tomasa didn't know what to make of his words. "Then why do you torment her?"

"At first I wanted to punish her, but I don't care about that now. You visit me because she's sick," he said with a shy smile. "I want you to keep visiting me."

Tomasa felt those words like a blow. Shock mingled with anger and a horrible, dangerous pleasure that rendered her almost incapable of speech. "I won't come again," she shouted.

"You will," said the *enkanto*. He pulled himself up onto a branch of the tree, then hooked his foot in the back and climbed higher, to where the thick green leaves hid him from view.

"I will never forgive you." Tomasa meant to shout it, but it came out of her mouth in a whisper. There was no reply but the gentle night breeze and distant radio.

Her hands were shaking. She looked down at them and saw the loop of gold chain still dangling from her fingers.

And suddenly—just like that—she had a plan. An impossible, absurd plan. She made a fist around the gold pendant, feeling its edges dig into her palm. Her feet found their way over brush and vine as she darted through the town to the tamarind tree.

The elf was sitting on one of the boughs when she got there. His eyebrows rose slightly, but he smiled. She smiled back.

"I've been rude," she said, hoping that when he looked at her he would think the guilt in her eyes was for what she'd done, not for what she was about to do. "I'm sorry."

He jumped down, one arm touching the trunk to steady him. "I'm glad you came."

Tomasa walked closer. She put one hand where the old man had bitten him, hoping that he wouldn't notice her other hand was fisted. "How's your arm?"

"Fine," he said. "Weak. I can move it a little now."

Steeling herself, she looked up into his face and slid her hand higher on his arm, over his shoulder and to his neck. His green eyes narrowed.

"What are you doing?" he asked. "You're acting strange."

"Am I?" She searched for some passable explanation. "Maybe the potion hasn't really worn off."

He shook his head. His black hair rustled against her arm, making her shiver.

She slid her other hand to his throat, twining both around his back of his neck.

He didn't push her away, although his body went rigid.

Then, as quick as she could, she wrapped the chain around his neck like a golden garrote.

He choked once as she clasped the necklace. Then she stepped back, stumbling on the roots of the tamarind. His hands flew to his throat but stopped short of touching the gold.

"What have you done?" he demanded.

She crouched down in the dirt, scuttling back from him. "Release my sister from your curse." Her voice sounded cold, even to her. In truth, she didn't know what she'd done.

"It is my right! She insulted me." The elf swallowed hard around the collar.

Insulted him? Tomasa almost laughed. Only an elf would let one girl stab his tree but curse another for being insulting. "I won't take the chain off your neck unless you make her well."

The *enkanto's* eyes flashed with anger.

"Please," Tomasa asked.

He looked down. She could no longer read his expression. "She'll be better when you get home," he muttered.

She crept a little closer. "How do I know you're telling the truth?"

"Take it off me!" he demanded.

Tomasa wanted to say something else, but the words caught in her throat as she reached behind his neck and unhooked the chain. She knew she should run. She'd beaten him and if she stayed any longer, he would surely put a curse on her. But she didn't move.

He watched her for a moment, both of them silent. "That was—" he said finally.

"Definitely bad luck," she offered.

He laughed at that, a short soft laugh that made her cheeks grow warm. "You really wanted me to come and visit?"

"I *did*," he said with a snort.

She grinned shyly. Balling up the necklace in her hand, she tossed it in the direction of the stream.

"You know," he said, taking one of her wrists and placing it on his shoulder. "Before, when you had your hand right here, I thought that you were going to kiss me."

Her face felt hot. "Maybe I wish I had."

"It's not too late," he said.

His lips were sour, but his mouth was warm.

By the time that Tomasa got home, the sky was pink and birds were screeching from their trees. Eva was already awake, sitting at the breakfast table, eating a plate of eggs. She looked entirely recovered.

"Where were you?" Rosa asked, refilling Eva's teacup. "Where's your pendant?"

Tomasa shrugged. "I must have lost it."

"I can't believe you stayed out all night." Eva gave her a conspiratorial smile.

"*Mananambal*," Rosa whispered as she returned to the kitchen. Tomasa almost stopped her to ask what she meant, but the truth made even less sense than anyone's guesses.

Upstairs, Tomasa picked up the crushed tamarind pod from her dresser. His words were still clear in her mind from that first meeting. *Whoever eats this will love you.* She looked into the mirror, at her birthmark, bright as blood, at her kiss-stung lips, at the absurd smile stretching across her face.

Carefully separating out the crushed pieces of shell, she pulled the dried pulp free from its cage of veins. Piece by piece, she put the sweet brown fruit in her own mouth and swallowed it down.

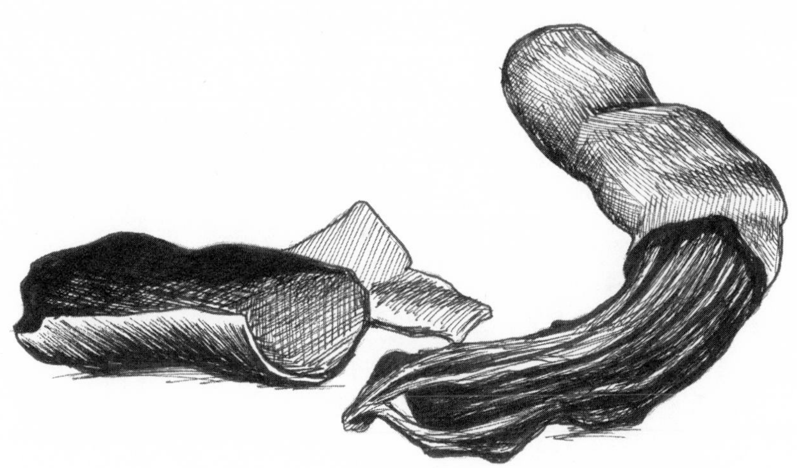

The Dog King

EVERY WINTER, HUNGER DRIVES the wolves out of the mountains of Arn and they sweep across the forests outlying the northern cities. They hunt in packs as large as armies and wash over the towns in their path like a great wave might crash down on hills of sand. Villagers may board up their windows and build up their fires, but the wolves are clever. Some say that they can rise up on two legs and speak as men, that nimble fingers can chip away at hinges, that their voices can call promises and pleas through keyholes, that they are not quite what they seem.

When whole towns are found empty in the spring, doors ajar, bed linens smeared with dirt and fur, cups and plates still on the tables, white bones piled in the hearth, people say these things and many other things besides.

But in the city of Dunbardain, behind the high walls and iron gates, ladies wear bejeweled wolf toes to show boldness and advertise fecundity. Men have statues of wolves commissioned to grace their parlors. And everyone cheers for wolves at the dog fights. City people like to feel far from the little towns and their empty, dirt-smeared beds.

Each year, wolves are caught in traps or, very occasionally, a litter is discovered and they are brought to the city to die spectacularly. Arn wolves are striking, black and slim as demons, with the unsettling habit of watching the audience as they tear out the throats of their opponents. City dwellers are made to feel both uneasy and inviolable by the dog fights; the caged wolf might be terrible, but it is caged. And the dog fights are majestic tented affairs, with the best bred dogs from all parts of the world as challengers. Expensive and exotic foods perfume the air, lulling one into the sense that danger is just another alluring spice.

Not to be outdone by his subjects, the king of Dunbardain obtained his own wolf pup and has trained it to be his constant companion. He calls it Elienad. It is quite a coup to have one, not unlike making the son of a great foreign lord one's slave. The wolf has very nice manners, too. He rests beneath the king's table, eats scraps of food daintily from the king's hand, and lets the ladies of the court ruffle his thick, black fur.

The velvet drapes of the tablecloth hang like bedcurtains around the wolf, who lolls there among the satin and bejeweled slippers of courtiers and foreign envoys.

Under the table of the king is a place of secrets. Letters are passed, touches are given or sometimes taken, silverware is stolen, and threats are made there, while above the table everyone toasts and grins. But the king has a secret too.

The wolf watches and his liquid eyes take it all in. This dark place is nothing to the magnificent glittering ballrooms or even the banquet hall itself with its intricate murals and gilt candelabras, but here is his domain. He knows the lore of under the table and could recite it back to anyone who asked, although only one person ever does.

A woman sitting beside Lord Borodin reaches her hand down. A fat ruby glistens as she holds out a tiny wing of quail. Grease slicks her fingers.

Once, Elienad took a bitter-tasting rasher of bacon from Lord Nikitin and was sick for a week. He knows he should learn from that encounter, but the smell of the food makes his mouth water and he takes the wing as gently as he can. The tiny bones crunch easily between his teeth, filling his mouth with the taste of salt and marrow. It wakes his appetite, makes his stomach hurt with the desire to tear, to rend. The woman allows him to lick her hand clean.

There is a boy who lives in the castle of Dunbardain, although no servant is quite sure in which room he sleeps. He dresses too shabbily to be a nobleman's son; he does not wear the livery of a page nor has he the rags of a groom. His tutors are scholars who have been disgraced or discredited: drunks and lunatics who fall asleep during his lessons. His hair is too long and his breeches are too tight. No one has any idea who his mother is or why he is allowed to run wild in a palace.

When they start dying, it is the master of the dog fights who is first accused. After all, if he allowed one of the wolves to get free, he should have let the guard know. But he claims that all his wolves are chained in their cages and offers to show anyone who doesn't believe him. Even as he stands over the body of the first child, with her guts torn out of her body and gobbets bitten out of her flesh, he argues that it can't be one of his wolves.

"Look at all these partial bites," he says, pointing with a silver cane as he covers his nose with a scented handkerchief. "It didn't know how to kill. You think one of my wolves would win if they hesitated like that?"

His assistant, who is still young enough to become attached to the dogs when they are pups and cries himself to sleep when one of them dies, walks three steps off to vomit behind a hedgerow.

With the second child, there are no hesitation marks, nor with the third or the fourth. Stories of dark, liquid shapes outside windows and whispers through locks spread through the city like a fever.

"Whosoever kills the beast," the king proclaims, "he will rule after me."

There are a group of knights there at the announcement, one of whom the king favors. The king knew Toran's father and has watched over the boy as he grew into the fierce-looking young man standing before him. Toran has killed wolves before, in the north. Everyone knows the king hopes it will be Toran who kills this wolf and takes the crown.

As the others are leaving, Toran walks toward the king. The king's wolf bares his teeth and makes a sound, deep in his throat. The knight hesitates.

"Stop that, Elienad," the king says, knocking his knee into the wolf's muzzle. Courtiers stare. Everyone thinks the same thought and the king knows it, flushes.

"He is always with you, is he not?" Toran asks. The king narrows his eyes, furious, until he realizes that Toran is giving him a chance to speak without a protestation seeming like a sign of guilt.

"Of course he is," says the king. "With me or locked up." This is not true, but he says it with such authority that it seems true. Besides, the courtiers will tell one another, later, when the king is gone. Besides, the king's wolf would be seen slipping back into the palace. The king's wolf would surely have killed a nearby child. The killer could not be the wolf they have fed and cosseted and stroked.

Elienad sits, chews on the fur around one paw like it itches. His gaze rests on the ground.

Toran nods, unsure about whether he should have spoken. The king nods too, once, with a slight smile.

"Walk with me," the king says.

The two men walk together down one of the labyrinthine hallways with the wolf trotting close behind.

"It is time to send him away," the king's chamberlain says softly. He is old and always chilled; he sits close to the fire, rubbing his knuckles as though he is washing his hands over and over again. "Or fight him. He'd make a good fighter."

"Elienad hasn't killed anyone," the king says. "And he's useful. You can't deny that."

The chamberlain served the king's father and used to give the king certain looks when he was being a particularly obstinate child. The chamberlain gives him one of those looks now.

The king is no longer a child. He pours himself more wine and waits.

"Only commoners have been killed, yet," the chamberlain finally says with an exasperated sigh. "Were a noble to die and it to come to light just what it is you've been keeping—"

The king takes a long drink from his cup.

The old man looks at the fire. "You should never have kept him for so long. It has only become harder to part with him."

"Yes," the king said softly. "He is nearly grown."

"And those tutors. I have always said it was too great a risk. And for what? So he can write down the things he overhears?"

"A well-informed spy is a better spy. He understands what to listen for. Who to follow." The king rubs his mouth. He's tired. He wishes his chamberlain would leave.

"The story you told me, years back, when you brought him here. Tell me again that it was the truth. That you didn't know what he was when you bought him. *That* you bought him."

The king is silent.

He does not know that his wolf lies on the cold stone outside of the door, letting the chill seep up into his heart.

The boy's room is hidden behind curtains and a bookcase that shifts to one side. Only a very few people know how to find it. Inside the room is a carved bed, a boy's bed, and now Elienad has to bend his knees to fit his legs inside it. There are no windows and no candles, but his liquid eyes see as well here as they do beneath the table or in the labyrinth of the castle.

When the king comes in, he opens the bookshelf and lets

light flood the little room. "What did you learn?" he asks.

"The pretty woman with the curls. Her name starts with an A, I think, and she likes to wear purple. She wants to poison her husband." As he speaks, the boy carves a small block of wood. He has skill; the king can make out the beginning of a miniature crest.

"Who taught you how to do that?" the king demands, pointing to the knife.

Elienad shrugs slender shoulders. "No one."

Which seems unlikely, but there is no reason for that to bother the king. Yet it does. The boy has recently turned thirteen and when the king thinks back on that age, he remembers telling many lies. Elienad's jaw looks firmer than it did a year ago, his soft limbs turning into the lean, hard arms of an adult. Soon the king will know even less about what he does.

"Does she mean to do it?" he asks, "or is it just talk?"

"Amadine," the boy says. "I remember her name now. She's bought powder and honey to hide the taste. She says it will seem like he's getting sick. Her friends are very proud of her. They say they are too frightened to kill their own husbands."

The boy looks up at him, hesitating, and the king thinks that if Elienad were a human boy, it would be abominable to raise him as a spy with no companions save drunk scholars and the king himself.

"Go on," the king says. "You have something else to tell me?"

The boy tilts his head to one side. His hair has gotten long. "Who was my mother?"

"I don't know," says the king, shaking his head. The boy asked for this story over and over again when he was very young, but he hasn't asked in a long time. "I've told you how you were brought to me by hunters and I bought you from them."

"Because I licked your hand," the boy said. "I was the last of a litter. The other pups died of exposure."

The king nods slowly; there is something new in the boy's voice, something calculating.

"That's not a true story," he says.

The king thinks he should be angry, but what he feels is panic. "What do you mean?"

The boy is very calm, very still. "I could hear it in your voice. It isn't a true story, but I can't tell which parts are false."

"You will not question me," the king commands, standing. "I will not be questioned." He thinks of Elienad, lying beneath tables, listening to the inflections of lies. Watching the hesitations, the gestures, the tensed muscles. Learning a language the king was unaware he even spoke.

"Did my brothers and sisters go to the fights?" the boy asks and his voice hitches a little. He drops the wood and the knife on the bed and stands. "Was it you who found me? Maybe you shot my mother? Please just tell me."

The king is too afraid to answer, afraid some movement will give him away. He stalks from the room. When he looks back, Elienad has not followed him.

"I won't be mad," the boy says softly as the door shuts.

The king's heart is beating so loudly that he thinks everyone in the hall must hear it. To him, the sound is the dull thudding of something chasing him, something that speeds the faster he runs from it.

Late that night, the boy leaves his room and pads barefoot to the great hall where the throne is. He sits on the velvet and runs his hands over the carved wood. He imagines himself no longer cowering under a table. He imagines looking every one of the courtiers in the eye.

Every evening the knights ride out into the town and hunt. They patrol the streets until dawn and come back empty-handed.

One night as the courtiers spin in a complicated dance that looks like cogs in a delicate machine, Toran walks into court, his armor wet and red. At the sight of the blood, ladies shriek and the wheels of spinning dancers come apart.

The king is flushed with exertion. "How dare you?" he demands, but Toran seems to ignore him, sinking down on one knee.

"The monster attacked me," the knight says, his head still bowed. "We fought and I managed to slice off one of its paws."

He opens a stained woven bag, but inside is no gory paw. Instead there is a slim hand with long, delicate fingers, pale save for the hacked flesh and severed bone at one end. And one finger is circled with a fat ruby ring.

There are more screams. Elienad smells blood and fear and the commingling of those scents wakes something coiled inside of him.

Toran drops the bag, rises, backs away. "Your majesty," he stammers.

Elienad pads closer. Courtiers shrink from him.

"This hand came from a wolf?" the king asks, still hoping that somehow it has not come to this.

One of Toran's party, all of whom idle near the doorway, not bold enough to interrupt the king, steps forward. "It was. We all saw it. That thing killed Pyter."

"The rumors are all true! The creatures walk among us!" Lady Mironov says, before swooning to the floor. She is practiced at swooning and is caught easily by her husband and his brother.

"It is gravely wounded," says the king. "It will be tracked and destroyed." He hopes it will be killed before it can be interrogated. He does not want to hear the things of which the creature might speak. His kingdom must have the illusion of safety, even at the cost of truth.

He does not remember the ring or the woman who wore it, but Elienad does. He recognizes the red stone and remembers the hand he licked clean under the table.

Elienad finds her by smell, behind Lord Borodin's stables. The horses shift and whinny in their pens as he passes. Her blood has soaked the icy ground around her and dotted the snow with bright red holes, like someone scattered poisonous berries. She is wrapped in a horse blanket, stiff with gore. Her hair is tangled with dirt and twigs.

She has never seen him with a human face, but she knows him immediately. Her pale mouth curves into a smile. "I didn't know they let you out of the palace," she says. She is very beautiful, even dying.

"They don't," he says and knees beside her. "Give me your arm."

He ties his sash around it as tightly as he can and the bleeding ebbs. It is probably too late, but he does it anyway.

"It is a hunger never ending, to be what we are. It gnaws at my stomach." Her eyes look strange, her pupils blown wide and black.

"Where did you come from?" he asks her. He doesn't want to talk about the hunger, not with the smell of her blood making him dizzy.

"From the forests," she says. "They caught my son. I thought it would be easy to find him. I had never even seen a city."

He can't help hoping. "Like me. They brought me—"

She sees his face and laughs. It is a thin rattling sound. "He's dead. And you never came from any forest."

"What do you mean?" he asks. He has brought a sack with men's clothes. They are too loose for her in some places and too tight in others, but they are warm and dry.

She struggles to get the shirt over her head. Her shoulders are shaking with cold. "You were born here, in this city. Didn't you know?"

"I don't understand." Part of him wishes she would stop talking because he feels as he does when he's about to shift, like he's drowning. The rest of him only wishes she would speak faster.

"A mirror would tell you more than I could." Her sly look bothers him, but he still doesn't know what she means.

He shakes off the questions. "We have to get you inside. Somewhere warm."

"No. I can care for myself." Her hand slides under her body. She holds out a knife. Toran's knife. "I want you to take this and put it into the chest of the king."

His eyes narrow.

"Have you been to the dog fights? Have you seen how we are set against each other, how we are kept in stinking pens?"

"You murdered those children," he says softly. "And then you ate them."

"Let them know what it is to have their babies snatched from them, what it is to be afraid and then find that they were killed for amusement. *For amusement.*" Her face is so pale that it looks like the snow. "You are not the only wolf he has kept, but the first one was grown when he got her. She died rather than become his pet. You are nothing but an animal to him."

"I see," he says. "Yes, you are right." Elienad takes the knife from her cold hand. He looks at his face in its mirrored surface and his features look as though they belong to someone else. His voice is only a whisper. "He must think I am an animal."

The king leaves his court late and stumbles tipsily to his rooms. The court will continue to celebrate until they collapse beneath tables, until they have drunk themselves so full of relief that they are sick from it.

The king lights a lamp on his desk and begins to write the speech he will give in the morning. He plans to say many reassuring things. He plans to declare Toran his heir.

He hears a laugh. It is a boy's laugh.

"Elienad?" the king asks the darkness.

There is silence, then the sound of laughter again, naughty and close.

"Elienad," the king says sternly.

"I will be king after you," the boy says.

The king's hands begin to shake so hard that the ink on his pen nib spatters the page. He looks down at it as though the wet black marks will tell him what to do now.

The boy moves into the lamplight, his face lit with an impish smile, showing white teeth.

"Please," says the king.

"Please what, Father?" The boy blows down the glass of the lamp and the light goes out.

In the darkness, the king calls the boy's name for the third time, but his voice quavers. He remembers his age, remembers how stiff he is from dancing.

This time when he hears the boy's laughter, it is near the door. He hears the footsteps as bare feet slap their way out the door and down the dark hall. Like the court, the king feels sick with relief.

Later, when the king lights the lamps—all of them—he will think of another woman, now long gone, and of her liquid eyes staring up at him in the dark. He will not sleep.

In the morning, he will make his way to the throne room. There, he will find courtiers gathered around a young boy with black hair in need of cutting. Beside the boy will be a corpse. The dead woman's hand will be missing and her throat will be cut. Dimly, the king will remember that he promised the kingdom to whosoever killed the wolf. And the boy will smile up at him as the trap closes.

Virgin

LET ME TELL YOU something about unicorns—they're faeries and faeries aren't to be trusted. Read your storybooks. But maybe you can't get past the rainbows and pastel crap. That's your problem.

Zachary told me once why the old stories say that mortals who eat faerie food can't leave Faerie. That's a bunch of rot, too, but at least there's some truth in it. You see, they *can* leave; they just won't ever be able to find another food they'll want to eat. Normal food tastes like ashes. So they starve. Zachary should have listened to his own stories.

I met him the summer I was squatting in an old building with my friend Tanya and her boyfriend. I'd run away from my last foster family, mostly because there didn't seem to be any point in staying. I was humoring myself into thinking I could live indefinitely like this.

Tanya had one prosthetic leg made from this shiny pink plastic stuff; so she looked like she was part Barbie doll, part girl. She loved to wear short, tight skirts and platform shoes to show off her leg. She knew the name of every boy who hung out in LOVE park. Tanya introduced us.

My first impression of Zachary was that he was a beautiful junkie. He wasn't handsome; he was pretty, the kind of boy that girls draw obsessively in the corners of their notebooks. Tall, great cheekbones, and red-black hair rolling down the sides of his face in fat curls. He was juggling a tennis ball, a fork, and three spoons. A cardboard sign next to his feet had *will juggle anything for food* written on it in an unsteady hand. *Anything* had been underlined shakily, twice. Junkie, I thought. I wondered if Tanya had ever slept with him. I wanted to ask her what it was like.

After he was done and had collected a little cash in a paper cup, he walked around with us for a while, mostly listening to Tanya tell him about her band. He had a bag over his shoulder and walked solemnly, hands in the pockets of his black jeans. He didn't look at her, although sometimes he nodded along with what she was saying, and he didn't look at me. He bought us ginger beer with the coins people had thrown at him and that's when I knew he wasn't a junkie, because no junkie who looked as hard up as he did would spend his last quarters on anything but getting what he needed.

The next time I saw Zachary, it was at the public library. We would all go there when we got cold. Sometimes I would go alone to read sections of *The Two Towers,* jotting down the page where I stopped on the inside hem of my jeans. I found him sitting on the floor between the mythology and psychiatry shelves. He looked up when I started walking down the aisle and we just stared at one another for a moment, like we'd been found doing something illicit. Then he grinned and I grinned. I sat down on the floor next to him.

"Just looking," I said, "What are you reading?" I had just run half the way to the library and could feel the sweat on my scalp. I knew I looked really awful. He looked dry, even cold. His skin was as pale as if he never spent a day in the park.

He lifted up the book spread open across his lap: *Faerie Folktales of Europe.*

I was used to people who wouldn't shut up. I wasn't used to making conversation.

"You're Zachary, right?" I asked, like an asshole.

He looked up again. "Mmhmm. You're Jen, Tanya's friend."

"I didn't think you'd remember," I said, then felt stupid. He just smiled at me.

"What are you reading?" I stumbled over the words, realizing halfway through the sentence I'd already asked that. "I mean, what *part* are you reading?"

"I'm reading about unicorns," he said, "but there's not much here."

"They like virgins," I volunteered.

He sighed. "Yeah. They'd send girls into the woods in front of the hunts. Girls to lure out the unicorn, get it to lie down, to sleep. Then they'd ride up and shoot it or stab it or slice off its horn. Can you imagine how that girl must have felt? The sharp horn pressing against her stomach, her ears straining to listen for the hounds."

I shifted uncomfortably. I didn't know anyone who talked like that. "You looking for something else about them?"

"I don't even know." He tucked some curls behind one ear. Then he grinned at me again.

All that summer was a fever dream, restless and achy. He was a part of it, meeting me in the park, or at the library. I told him about my last foster home and about the one before that, the one that had been really awful. I told him about the boys I met and where we went to drink—up on rooftops. We talked about where pigeons spent their winters and where we were going to spend ours. When it was his turn to talk, he told stories. He told me ones I knew, old stories, and he told me old-sounding ones I had never heard. It didn't matter that I spent the rest of the week begging for cigarettes and hanging with hoodlums. When I was with Zachary, everything seemed different.

Then one day, when it was kind of rainy cold and we were scrounging in our pockets for money for hot tea, I asked him where he slept.

"Outside the city, near the zoo."

"It must stink." I found another sticky dime in the folds of my backpack and put it on the concrete ledge with our other change.

"Not so much. When the wind's right."

"So how come you live all the way out there? Do you live with someone?" It felt strange that I didn't know.

He put some lint-encrusted pennies down, and looked at me hard. His mouth parted a little and he looked so intent that for a moment, I thought he was going to kiss me.

Instead, he said, "Can I tell you something crazy? I mean totally insane."

"Sure. I've told you weird stuff before."

"Not like this. Really not like this."

"Okay," I said.

And that's when he told me about her. A unicorn. His unicorn. Who he lived with in a forest between two highways just outside the city. Who waited for him at night, and who ran free, hanging out with the forest animals or doing whatever it is unicorns do, all day long, while Zachary told me stories and scrounged for tea money.

"My mother . . . she was pretty screwed up. She sold drugs for some guys and then she sold information on those guys to the cops. So one day when this car pulled up and told us to get in, I guess I wasn't all that surprised. Her friend, Gina, was already sitting in the back and she looked like she'd been crying. The car smelled bad, like old frying oil.

"Mom kept begging them to drop me off and they kept silent, just driving. I don't think I was really scared until we got on the highway.

"They made us get out of the car near some woods and then walk for a really long time. The forest was huge. We were lost. I was tired; my mother dragged me along by my hand. I kept falling over branches. Thorns wiped along my face.

"Then there was a loud pop and I started screaming from the sound even before my mother fell. Gina puked."

I didn't know what to do, so I put my hand on his shoulder. His body was warm underneath his thin t-shirt. He didn't even look at me as he talked.

"There isn't much more. They left me alone there with my dead mom in the dark. Her eyes glistened in the moonlight. I wailed. You can imagine. It was awful. I guess I remember a lot, really. I mean, it's vivid but trivial.

"After a long time, I saw this light coming through the trees. At first I thought it was the men coming back. Then I saw the horn. Bleached bone. Amazing, Jen. So amazing. I lifted up my hand to pet her side and blood spread across her flank. I forgot everything but that moment, everything but the white pelt, for a long, long while. It was like the whole world went white."

His face was flushed. We bought one big cup of tea with tons of honey and walked in the rain, passing the cup between us. He moved more restlessly than usual but was quieter, too.

"Tell me some more, Zachary," I said.

"I shouldn't have said what I did."

We walked silently for a while 'til the rain got too hard and we had to duck into the foyer of a church to wait it out.

"I believe you," I said.

He frowned. "What's wrong with you? What kind of idiot believes a story like that?"

I hadn't really considered whether I believed him or not. Sometimes people just tell you things and you have to accept that *they* believe them. It doesn't always matter if they're true.

I turned away and lit a cigarette. "So you lied?"

"No, of course not. Can we just talk about something else for a while?" he asked.

"Sure," I said, searching for something good. "I've been thinking about going home."

"To your jerk of a foster father and your slutty foster sisters?"

"The very ones. Where am I going to stay come winter otherwise?"

He mulled that over for a few minutes, watching the rain pound some illegally parked cars.

"How 'bout you squat libraries?" he said, grinning.

I grinned back: "I could find an elderly, distinguished gentlemanly professor and totally throw myself at him. Offer to be his Lolita."

We stood awhile more before I said, "Maybe you should hang with people, even if they're assholes. You could stay with me tonight."

He shook his head, looking at the concrete.

And that was that.

I told Tanya about Zachary and the unicorn that night, while we waited for Bobby Diablo to come over. Telling it, the story became a lot funnier than it had been with Zachary's somber black eyes on mine. Tanya and I laughed so hard that I started to choke.

"Look," she said. "Zach's entertainingly crazy. Everybody loves him. But he's craz-*az*-azy. Like last summer, he said that he could tell if it was going to rain by how many times he dropped stuff." She grinned. "Besides, he looks like a girl."

"And he's into unicorns." I thought about how I'd felt when I thought he was about to kiss me. "Maybe I like girly."

She pointed to a paperback of *The Hobbit* with a dragon on the torn remains of the cover. "Maybe you like crazy."

I rolled my eyes.

"Seriously," she said. "Reading that stuff would depress me. People like us—we're not in those kind of books. They're not *for* us."

I stared at her. It might have been the worst thing anybody had ever said to me.

Because no matter how much I thought about it, I couldn't make it feel any less true.

But when I was around Zachary, it had seemed possible that those stories were for me. Like it didn't matter where I came from, like there was something heroic and special and magical about living on the street. Right then, I hated him for being crazy. Hated him more than I hated Tanya, who was just pointing out the obvious.

"What do you think really happened?" I asked, finally, because I had to say something eventually. "With his mom? Why would he tell me a story about a *unicorn*?"

She shrugged. She wasn't big on introspection. "He just needs to get laid."

Later on, while Bobby Diablo tried to put his hands up Tanya's halter top before her boyfriend came back from the store and I tried to pretend I didn't hear her giggling yelps, while the whiskey burned my throat raw and smooth, I had a black epiphany. There were rules to things, even to delusions. And if you broke those rules, there were consequences. I lay on the stinking rug and breathed in cigarette smoke and incense, measuring out my miracle.

The next afternoon, I left Tanya and her boyfriend tangled around one another. The cold grey sky hung over me. Zachary was going to hate me, I thought, but that only made me walk faster through the gates to the park. When I finally found him, he was throwing bits of bread to some wet rats. The rodents scattered when I got close.

"I thought those things were bold as hustlers," I said.

"No, they're shy." He tossed the remaining pieces in the air, juggling them. Each throw was higher than the last.

"You're a virgin, aren't you?"

He looked at me like I'd hit him. The bits of bread kept moving though, as if his hands were separate from the rest of him.

That night I followed Zachary home. Through the winding, urine-stained tunnels of the subway and the crowded trains themselves, always one car behind, watching him through the milky, scratched glass between the cars. I followed him as he changed trains; I hid behind a newspaper like a cheesy TV cop. I followed him all the way from the park through the edge of a huge cemetery where the stink of the zoo carried in the breeze. By then, I couldn't understand how he didn't hear me rustling behind him, the newspaper long gone and me hiking up my backpack every ten minutes. But Zachary doesn't exactly live in the here and now, and for once I had to be glad for that.

Then we came to a patch of woods and I hesitated. It reminded me of where my foster family lived, where the trees always seemed a menacing border to every strip mall. There were weird sounds all around and it was impossible to walk quietly. I forced myself to crunch along behind him in the very dark dark.

Finally, we stopped. A thick bunch of branches hung like a dome in front of him, their leaves dragging on the forest floor.

I couldn't see anything much under it, but it did seem like there was a slight light. He turned, either reflexively, or because he had heard me after all, but his face stayed blank. He parted the branches with his hands and ducked under them. My heart was beating madly in my chest, that too-much-caffeine drumming. I crept up and tried not to think too hard, because right then I wished I was in Tanya's apartment, watching her snort whatever, the way you're supposed to wish for mom's apple pie.

I wasn't cold; I had brought Tanya's boyfriend's thick jacket. I fumbled around in the pocket and found a big, dirty knife, which I opened and closed to make myself feel safer. I thought about walking back, but if I got lost I would absolutely have freaked out. I though about going under the branches into Zachary's house, but I didn't know what to expect and for some reason that scared me more than the darkness.

He came out then, looked around and whispered, "Jen."

I stood up. I was so relieved that I didn't even hesitate. His eyes were red-rimmed, like he had been crying. He extended one hand to me.

"God, it's scary out here," I said.

He put one finger to his lips.

He didn't ask me why I'd followed him; he just took my hand and led me further into the forest. When we stopped, he just looked at me. He swallowed like his throat was sore. This was my idea, I reminded myself.

"Sit down," I said and smiled.

"You want me to sit?" He sounded reassuringly like himself.

"Well, take off your pants first."

He looked at me incredulously, but he started to do it.

"Underwear too," I said. I was nervous. Oh boy, was I nervous. Mostly I had been drunk all the times before, or I had done what was expected of me. Never, never had I seduced a boy. I started to unlace my work boots.

"I can't," he said, looking toward the faint light.

"You don't want to?" I took one of his hands and set it on my hip.

His fingers dug into my skin, pulling me closer.

Why are you doing this?" His voice sounded husky.

I didn't answer; I couldn't. It didn't seem to matter anyway. His hands—those juggling hands that didn't seem to care what he was thinking—fumbled with the buttons of my jeans. We didn't kiss. He didn't close his eyes.

Leaves rustled and I could smell that rich, wet, storm smell in the air. The wind picked up around us.

Zachary looked up at me and then past my face. His features stiffened. I turned and saw a white horse with muddy hooves. For a moment, it seemed funny. It was just a horse. Then she bolted. She cut through the forest so fast that all I could see was a shape, a cutout of white paper, still running.

I could feel his breath on my mouth. It was the closest our faces had ever been. His eyes stared at nothing, watching for another flash of white.

"Do you want to get your stuff?" I said, stepping back from him.

He shook his head.

"What about your clothes?"

"It doesn't matter."

"I'll get them," I said, starting for the tree.

"No, don't," he said, so I didn't.

"Let's go back." I said.

He nodded, but he was still looking after where she had run.

We walked back, through the forest and then the graveyard, back, back to the comforting stink of urine and cigarettes. Back to the sulfur of buses that run all night; back to people who hassle you because you forgot your work boots in the enchanted forest where you cursed your best friend to live a life as small as your own.

I brought Zachary back to Tanya's. She was used to extra people crashed out there, so she didn't pay us any mind. Besides, Bobby was over. That night Zachary couldn't eat much, and what he did eat wouldn't stay down. I watched him, bent over her toilet, puking his guts out. After, he sat by the window, watching the swirling patterns of traffic while I huddled in the corner, letting numbness overtake me. Bobby and Tanya were rolling on the floor, wrestling. Finally Bobby pulled off Tanya's shorts right in front of the both of us. Zachary watched them in horrified fascination. He just stared. Then he started to cry, just a little, in his fist.

I fell asleep sometime around that.

When I woke up, he was juggling books, making them seem like they were flying. Tanya came in and gave him a tiny, plastic unicorn.

"Juggle this," she said.

He dropped the books. One hit me on the shin, but I didn't make a sound. When he looked at me, his face was empty. As if he wasn't even surprised to be betrayed. I felt sick.

Three days he lived with me there. Bobby taught him how to roll a joint perfectly and smoke without coughing. Tanya's boyfriend let him borrow his old guitar and Zachary screwed around with it all that second day. He laughed when we did, but always a little late, as though it was an afterthought. The next night, he told me he was leaving.

"But the unicorn's gone," I said.

"I'll find her."

"You're going to hunt her? Like one of those guys in the tapestries?" I tried to keep my voice from shaking. "She doesn't want you anymore."

He shook his head, but he didn't look at me. Like I was the crazy one. Like I was the one with the problem.

I took a deep breath. "Unicorns don't exist. I saw her. She was a horse. A white horse. She didn't have a horn."

"Of course she did," he said and kissed me. It was a quick kiss, an awful kiss really—his teeth bumped mine and his lips were chapped—but I still remember every bit of it.

That fall, I took my stuff and went back to my foster home. They yelled at me and demanded to know where I'd been, but in the end they let me stay. I didn't tell them anything. I went back to school sometime around Halloween. I still read a lot, but now I'm careful about the books I choose. I don't let myself think about Zachary. I turn on the television. I turn it up loud. I force my dinner out of cardboard boxes and swallow it down. Never mind that it turns to ash in my mouth.

In Vodka Veritas

WALLINGFORD PREPARATORY HAS TWO tracks. One is for kids who want to get into the good colleges that private boarding schools—even ones in New Jersey—are supposed to help you get into. The other track—the one not mentioned in the brochures—is for rich kids kicked out of public schools. It's probably been that way since before they let the girls in, back when this place was just the one building that's boarded up on the edge of the campus. Put on a jacket and tie every day and all sins are forgiven.

I've been at Wallingford five years—since I got expelled from the seventh grade for making a knife in metal shop. But I wasn't being psycho like the girls here think. If some asshole jock threatens to jump me after school because I made him look stupid in homeroom, I'm not going to just take the beating like a good little geek. My skinny ass wouldn't have exactly won in a fair fight, so I didn't play fair.

My mother says that I don't think about consequences until it's too late. That might be true.

But seriously, most of the reasons why Wallingford girls

think I'm crazy are stupid rumors. Like it wasn't my fault that after the school trip to France, everybody said I brought back the head of some guy who got into a motorcycle accident on the Rue Racine. Come on, anybody who believes that is a moron! How would I have gotten a head through customs? They won't even let in some Anjou pears. And painting my fingernails black is a cosmetic choice, not a symbol of my eternal devotion to Satan. It's also one of the only things I can do to get around the dress code—make-up is allowed and the handbook doesn't specify only on girls.

Yeah, so I guess you picked up on my lack of school pride. Want to know what Wallingford is really like? Each year, they have a fundraiser to restore Smythe Hall—that boarded-up eyesore I mentioned earlier—and each year the only thing that gets built is an addition on the Dean's house. That's also why we have to have our prom in our own banquet room. Sure, it's better than a gymnasium, but the public school kids get to dance and eat rubbery chicken in the ballroom of a Marriott.

It's not like I don't do any extracurricular activities, though. I'm the founder and president of the Wallingford gaming club—The Pawns. Our shtick is to break into empty classrooms and project Playstation games on the whiteboard or jerry-rig Doom 3 tournaments with our laptops. Sometimes we even go old-school and play paper-and-dice Dungeons and Dragons. It's my job to decide. That pretty much makes me Lord of the Losers. Which is great if you want a Phantom Blade with a Fiery Enchantment, but not so great if what you want is a date to the prom.

Luckily, my best friend, Danny Yu, V.P. and secretary of the Pawns, doesn't have a date either. There are many reasons why I love Danny, but the biggest one is that he's the only person at Wallingford as crazy as me.

Like one time, when he was home sick, he saw some daytime talk show that had a bunch of KKK members on and gave out the official website. So Danny flips open his laptop and sends them an email: *I am very interested in starting my own chapter of the Klan. Can you tell me what thread-count sheets we should wear?* A half hour later, he sends another one from a different account: *Do you believe that white bread is racially superior to other breads?* They never emailed him back.

Come on, you can't blame that shit on DayQuil. That's plain genius.

So it's the week before prom and we've already been shot down a couple of times. We're in Latin class and we're supposed to be translating something about Dionysus. He's going over our seriously limited choices instead.

"I could ask Daria Wisniewski," he says. "She likes comics."

"She has that creepy doll with the goggles she takes everywhere. Odds on her putting it in a matching prom dress and bringing it along."

"It could be your date, then," Danny says. "Perfect."

"What about Abby Goldstein?" I list off the reasons this is a good idea on my fingers. "Hot. Redhead. Talked to me twice without actually needing to."

"Dude, she'd never go out with you. Not even if she had a nasty fetish and you were the only one discreet and desperate enough to take care of it."

"Very vivid—that fantasy of yours. Weird that it's about me, though."

"Boys," says Ms. Esposito. She's tiny, shorter than a sixth-grader, but not someone you want to piss off. She drinks coffee all day long out of a thermos that has a French press built right into it. "How about you tell me what the Bacchanalia were?"

I stutter something, but Danny turns nonchalantly on his chair and smiles his most ass-kissing grin. "The festivals of Bacchus, called Dionysius by the Greeks. People got drunk and had big orgies."

Some of the class laughs, but not Ms. Esposito. "He was called Dionysius by the Romans and Bacchus by the Greeks, but otherwise essentially correct. Now, can anyone tell me what the Maenads were?"

We can't.

"No? Well, if we're going to continue reading the story of Orpheus, it's important to know. It was said that the mysteries of Bacchus inspired women into an ecstatic frenzy that included intoxication, fornication, bloodletting, and even mutilation. They would tear those not engaged in celebrating Bacchus limb from limb."

The class is silent.

"Xavier, can you read the first paragraph in Latin?" Ms. Esposito asks. She looks satisfied, like she knows she can freak us more than we can freak her. As Xavier starts to read, Danny turns to me.

"Let's not go," he says.

I'm still thinking about wild women, streaked with mud and dried, black gore. In my mind, it's kind of hot. "What?"

"Let's get into our rented tuxes, take pictures with our parents, pretend we're off to get our dates, score a bottle of booze and do something dumb, something different." His kiss-ass grin has not faded and I realize something about that smile. It's kind of smug. Charming but smug.

I'm torn. On one hand, it sounds like a pretty good plan. On the other hand, it's a plan I didn't come up with. "Let's break into Smythe Hall. Do some urban exploring right on campus."

"Genius." His grin widens into a smile and the naked, crazy girls fade from my mind.

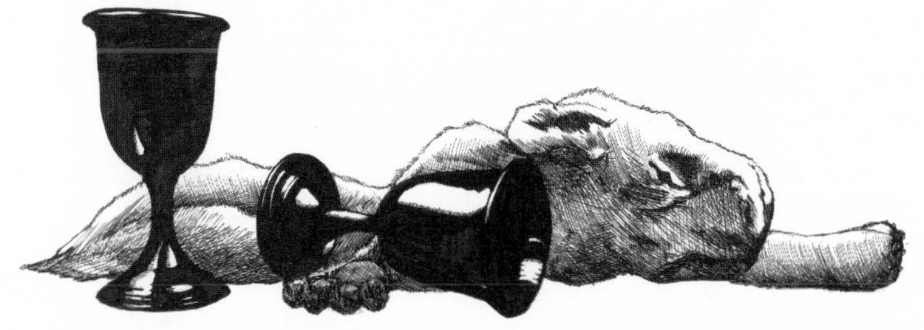

The night before we're supposed to go, Danny calls me. "Um, dude. I feel like a dick, but I have a date. I'm going to the prom."

I'm in my dorm room, downloading torrented episodes of *Veronica Mars* and googling the old school. I was going to tell him that there were photos on Weird NJ of the place. I was going to tell him that supposedly someone remembered having a prom there. I had maps and everything printing in color off my inkjet.

My hamster, Snot, runs on his wheel and I hear only the clack, clack, clack of the wire because I'm not speaking. Snot's been hiding the choice bits of seeds from his food bowl for the last half hour but now he's finally decided to kick his night into high gear. Lucky him.

"Who?" I ask.

"Daria," he says. "She asked me, man. And she has a friend who could go with you—"

I don't wait to see who the spare friend is that Daria Wisniewski's willing to throw in to sweeten the pot. I don't ask if it's her stupid doll. I just hang up the phone.

He calls back twice, but I just let the phone buzz. I look at the tuxedo hanging on the door of the closet. Inside, underneath the floorboard I pried up myself, is the half bottle of Grey Goose left from the ones I took from a pile of my parents' corporate gifts during the holiday break. Now it seems like there isn't nearly enough.

My roommate left for his dad's house this afternoon. He and his date are taking the SATs in the morning and then going straight to prom. I'm not sure if he thinks that's like foreplay or what. Anyway, I'm glad he's not here, because my eyes burn like I just got dumped.

I know I'm not supposed to cry over a guy standing me up. So I don't. But I have to practically break my knuckles against the brick wall outside my window to manage it.

By the time I get to the abandoned part of the school on prom night, I'm already drunk.

The good thing about living at a private school is that you already know how to break into places. You learn how to break into other guys' rooms to take their hot cocoa mix and soup cups. You learn how to break into unused classrooms because that's the only place you can really set up a bunch of computers for a tournament. If you're like Danny and me, you learn how to grappling hook out of your dorm room and break into the cafeteria because sometimes what you really need is a sandwich.

So, basically, I take off the hinges. No problem if you're sober, but it takes a while for me and I have to set down my bottle. Then I almost knock it over. It makes a hollow sound and scrapes over the concrete. I snatch it up by the neck and stumble inside, leaving the door just leaning there, sagging from the knob.

Inside, the dust is so thick that the cuffs of my pants are already white with it. The walls are wainscoted in wood, and along the water-streaked boards I see the outlines of where paintings once hung. I take another sip. The vodka no longer burns as it goes down. I feel like I'm drinking water.

I loosen my tie and a kind of giddiness comes over me. It's much cooler to be here than at the prom. I bet Danny forgot to get Daria a corsage and she's already resenting him. I bet they're taking stupid posed pictures in front of some kind of draped cloth and a vase full of red, red roses. I bet that the chicken is rubbery and the music is bad. I bet he's forgotten that we were going to wear tuxedos on our little breaking and entering expedition and had to rent whatever was left. I imagine him in light blue with a ruffled shirt. That makes me almost laugh out loud, but my smile turns sour when I realize that it would actually be *funny* and I see us both in them, exalting in our dorkitude.

Maybe I should have just sucked it up and taken the pity date. I wonder if Danny is pissed that I hung up on him, if he thinks that I'm afraid of girls. Suddenly, I'm morose. Being drunk by myself in an old building doesn't seem as edgy as it did moments before. It seems sad and a little pathetic.

Just then, I hear a sound down the hallway. I get up, clumsy with booze. My fingers and tongue are so numb that it's almost pleasurable to stumble. I know that it could be one of the rent-a-cops the school's probably crawling with or even one of the administrators but my drunk brain can't help conjuring up a girl. In my fantasy, she just got dumped by her jock boyfriend, she's stunningly beautiful, and she goes back to the prom with me on her arm.

I walk in the direction of the sound and I see candles flickering there. In the center of a large room, six robed figures funnel dark liquid into silver flasks. At their center is Ms. Esposito. I'm so surprised that it takes my brain long moments to catch up with what I'm seeing.

I stumble a little and they all look at me. The whole thing is so surreal that I start to laugh.

"*Ave,*" one of them says. I walk a little closer and I see Xavier. He's second board in the chess club, which makes him a member of the Pawns.

I salute him with my almost empty bottle of Grey Goose.

"*Potestatem obscuri lateris nescis,*" he said. Some of them laugh nervously.

I frowned, trying to figure out what he was saying. "Did you just tell me that I don't know the power of the dark side?" More laughter.

Xavier grins and turns to the others. "He's okay," he says. "He passed the test. Besides, I can vouch for him. He's down. And besides, *cornix cornici oculos non effodiet.*"

A crow doesn't rip out the eyes of another crow. Nice.

Looking at their faces, I suddenly realize I know them. It's the Latin Club. Diego, Jenny, Ashley, Mike, and David. And their advisor, Ms. Esposito. Geeks, one and all. My people.

"What are you doing?" My words come out slurred.

"Bringing Bacchanalia to Wallingford," said Jenny. "And you're going to help us."

I picture Jenny streaked with mud and blood, rolling around in an orgiastic frenzy, but the image doesn't stick.

"*Quomodo dicitur Latine*?" says Ms. Esposito.

I know that one. She wants Jenny to only talk in Latin.

"*Paenitere*," Jenny tells her.

It's then that I notice sequins at Ashley's throat under the robe and Mike's gleaming dress shoes. A crazy grin grows on my face as I realize they're wearing prom clothes. All this creepy shit aside, I finally get it. They're going to spike the punch. This is a prom prank of epic proportions.

Danny won't be part of it. He'll be slow-dancing like an idiot. He'll feel left out.

"*In vodka veritas*," I say and tilt back my bottle, pouring the last of it down my throat. I choke a little, but I swallow anyway. In vodka is the truth. I'm sure I declined that wrong.

Ms. Esposito doesn't smile, but she does hand me a vial of the whatever-it-is. I'm thinking Everclear. "*Nunc est bibendum*," she says. Now it's time to drink.

They snuff out their candles and strip off their robes near a closet. The gleaming wood and lack of dust points to them meeting here before, maybe lots of times.

"Wow," I say drunkenly to Xavier as we cross the quad. "This is pretty awesome. I had no idea Latin club was so cool." And I hadn't. I'd always pictured the Pawns as the big geek rebels. I'm actually a little intimidated. I kind of want to join.

He grins. "*Quidquid latine dictum sit, altum videtur.*"

That one takes me a while, but I finally figure it out. Everything's better when you say it in Latin. I restrain myself from rolling my eyes.

As we're about to enter the banquet hall, Mike turns to me and says, "*Cave quid dicis quando et cui.*" Basically, be careful what I say.

My plan is to be careful where I stand. I'm sure I stink of vodka and I bet that my eyes are glassy. Any advisor gets a whiff of me and I'm going to get hauled out of here.

"Look," Xavier says, leaning close to me, and I'm startled to hear him speak English. "The rest of them probably don't care what happens to you, but I want to make sure you understand. That stuff in the vial is an antidote. Take a quick sip and you won't be affected."

"But . . . aren't we just spiking the punch?" I ask.

He laughs. "No way. Look around. People are drinking water and soda and energy drinks. No one drinks punch out of a central punch bowl any more. That's out of some eighties movie."

I look around. The theme of the prom is Under the Sea. Blue, white, and gold streamers hang from the ceiling and the tables are covered in sea-green chiffon cloth. Someone has spray painted real shells gold and scattered them on the tables, hot-gluing them around napkin rings. Stenciled numbers mark the round tables. I think I see Danny across the room, sitting at one of them, next to Daria. He has his arm draped over her shoulders.

But Xavier's right. Servers are clearing plates of cake, but there's no table with a cake on it. No punch bowl beside it to spike. "Wait, so what are we doing exactly?"

"Dude, aren't you tired of the beautiful people lording over you?

Of course I'm tired of it. I nod.

He tilts his head toward the stage and the DJ. The shimmering lights of the dance floor reflect in the lenses of his glasses, obscuring his eyes. "They think they're so smart, but all they do is screw up, screw around, and screw off. Tonight, they'll see their own true natures. You'll love it. One steaming hot plate of revenge coming right up."

Across the room, I see Ms. Esposito lift her hands. She starts chanting and next to me, Xavier starts chanting too, with a wink in my direction. They're speaking low and I can't make out the words over the music. I feel weird, violent and too hot. I want to yell at Danny; I want to feel my knuckles bruise against his jaw.

Xavier smacks the side of my arm. I look at him and he's miming drinking something. I remember the vial in my pocket and take a sip. It tastes too sweet, like fortified wine. Immediately, I notice that I'm been breathing like I'm already in a fight. I shake my head. Everything's fine. I'm fine.

I turn toward the dance floor. Couples are grinding against one another, hands roaming over satin. Boys start unlacing their ties and shrugging off jackets. That's funny, I think.

Across the room, Jenny and Mike are leaving. Ashley takes a picture of the head master as he leans down to kiss Ms. Perez, our newest and youngest English teacher. Surprisingly, neither of them seem to notice the camera.

Behind me, Xavier laughs. I start walking toward where I saw Danny and Daria last.

Couples are no longer dancing—they're kissing and groping. A few have moved to lying on the floor together. The captain of the football team knocks the shells and plates off the table and throws Missy Carthage on it. He climbs on top of her.

It's all happening so fast. Someone hits someone else. I don't see how it starts, but there is a sudden knot of fighting.

The music has stopped and only human sounds fill the silence. The camera flashes again.

"What's happening?" someone asks. There's a girl in a shimmering green dress with one sleeve and a heavy ruffle on the bottom. Her hair is spiked up and saturated with glitter and her eyes are heavily outlined in black kohl, but her skin looks blotchy around the neck like she's getting hives. She slouches against the doorway.

She doesn't even go to this school.

"You should leave," I say, but then a boy catches her hand and pulls her into a kiss. She groans.

I grab her hand and pull her back to me. The boy lets her go and she slides into my arms. Her mouth comes against mine and we're kissing. I've only kissed three girls before and none of them kissed me like this, like they never wanted to stop, like they don't care about breathing. I pull back from her and she frowns, like she doesn't know where she is.

I shake my head, but that just makes me dizzy. The floor is carpeted in sequined gowns and black tuxedos. On top of them, bodies move together. I see the math teacher, Mr. Riggs, among them, writhing around with Jacob White and Nancy Chung.

Amy Gershwin's purple bra is around her waist, like a belt, as she crawls toward them.

Across the room, three cheerleaders corner another cheerleader and swipe at her with their long, manicured nails. Scratches mark both her cheeks.

I stumble forward and see Danny. He's lying half-underneath a table, kissing Hannah Davis, who turns and kisses Daria Wisniewski. None of them are very dressed. Hannah is wearing Wonder Woman underpants.

There's a part of me that figures Danny deserves whatever happens to him at that point. I know it's an asshole thing to think, but isn't this what he hoped would happen at one of the prom afterparties anyway? Would he really have turned down a threesome with two girls? I mean sure, everyone is going crazy, but aren't they just giving in to what they really desire? Isn't he?

And it's not like I could stop him.

Then I think of the vial in my pocket. There's still some liquid in it. But then, maybe he wouldn't want me to stop him.

"Danny," I say, still not sure. I want him to do something that will make him familiar again.

He turns toward me and his face is blank with desire.

I take out the vial, because I don't care what he wants or if he deserves it. I just want him to be Danny again.

"Drink some," I say, but he's kissing Daria and not paying any more attention. I get down on the floor. Someone is pulling off my jacket. I let it go.

Hannah Davis puts her lips to my neck and I reach over her to try and force Danny to drink, but everyone shifts and I'm afraid I'm going to spill the antidote.

So I take a swig and hold it in my cheek. I press my lips to his and when his mouth opens under mine, I spit it all out. Yes, okay, that's technically a kiss. Technically, I kissed Danny. But it worked.

"Dude," he says and stumbles to his feet. He looks like he just woke up out of a dream.

I have no idea what to say to him. "The Latin Club is totally evil," I blurt.

"The Latin Club?"

I can understand why he's confused.

"We have to stop them," I say, but they're not even here anymore. They've already succeeded, taken photographic evidence and gone home.

Danny picks up a pair of pants. Three kids are doing body shots off the limp body of the assistant headmaster. I don't even know where they got the liquor, but I think I see blood near his neck.

"What can we do?" he asks. Daria pulls at his pantleg and he stumbles, wide-eyed. "This is nuts."

"I know where they keep their stuff," I say and he follows me out of the banquet hall and out into the night. We run across campus to Smythe Hall. A few kids are out on the lawn, dancing around naked to the delight of the underclassmen hanging out the windows of their dorm.

Inside the abandoned building, I feel my way through the dusty rooms to the closet. My empty bottle of vodka is still there, but it looks unfamiliar, as though it's a relic from a hundred years ago.

The closet contains a moth-eaten lion cub skin, which is

both scary and gross, a bunch of goblets, and an almost-full bottle that smells and looks just like the antidote.

"I know what to do," I say and I explain my kiss/spit technique.

Danny raises his eyebrows higher than eyebrows should go. "Your plan is that we kiss everyone."

"Basically, yes," I say.

"Teachers included?" he asks.

I realize I'm looking at his mouth when he talks. I remember the way his lips feel. I'm a moron, but I think I get it. I finally get it.

"Everyone," I say. "Teachers. The basketball team. The administration. Hot girls. *Ev-er-y-one*."

He laughs. "It's genius," he says, "but definitely evil genius."

"Is there any other kind?" I quip.

So we kiss our way through the entire junior class. I make sure to plant a good one on the headmaster. It's pretty awesome to spit in his mouth.

When we're done, we round up Daria and Hannah and go out to a diner. We eat in silence, but Danny and I keep grinning at one another and finally we just start laughing, which the girls so don't appreciate.

"Sorry I was kind of a dick," I tell him after Daria and Hannah go back to their dorm. "And sorry we had to suck face to save the school."

"You're not sorry," he says and for a moment the words hang dangerously in the air, able to mean too many things. "You got to kiss Abby Goldstein," he finally finishes and we can both laugh.

"And you," I say, surprising myself. There I go, not thinking about consequences. I'm not even sure I know what I mean. No, I know what I mean.

"Yeah?" he asks.

I nod miserably. He knows what I mean too.

"That's cool," Danny says. "'Cause I'm such a stud, huh?"

"You're such an asshole," I say, but I laugh.

The next Monday is bizarre. Classes with juniors are almost entirely quiet. Lots of kids aren't even there. The underclassmen are buzzing like crazy with rumors. It's the first time I've ever seen knots of seniors, sophomores, and freshman, all gossiping together. Drugs, they're saying. A cult. It's kind of hilarious, except that people got hurt. The assistant administrator is still at the hospital, but his wife emailed his resignation.

I've got to admit it, I'm finding myself strangely full of Wallingford pride.

Of course, Mike and Xavier and all the rest of the Latin Club glare at me when we pass in the halls. I don't think they're all that mad though. Whatever blackmail scheme they got going is probably kicking into high gear. I'm sure they'll all be buying new computers by the end of the week.

Still, I'm a little nervous as I roll into Latin.

Danny's already there and he grins as I sit down next to him. "Dude," he says. "Want to go to Western Plaguelands tonight for a raid? I heard about a sunken temple in Caer Darrow with lots of purple drops."

"I'm on it like a bonnet," I say.

All things considered, he's a good best friend. Maybe better than me.

Ms. Esposito walks by my desk, holding her coffee. "*Antiquis temporibus, nati tibi similes in rupibus ventosissimis exponebantur ad nece,*" she says, which I think means that if we were back in the good old days, I'd be left out on a windswept crag to die.

She smiles.

I'm so registering for German next year.

The Coat of Stars

RAFAEL SANTIAGO HATED GOING home. Home meant his parents making a big fuss and a special dinner and him having to smile and hide all his secret vices, like the cigarettes he had smoked for almost sixteen years now. He hated that they always had the radio blaring salsa and the windows open and that his cousins would come by and try to drag him out to bars. He hated that his mother would tell him how Father Joe had asked after him at Mass. He especially hated the familiarity of it, the memories that each visit stirred up.

That morning he stood in front of his dressing table for half an hour, looking at the wigs and hats and masks—early versions or copies of costumes he'd designed. There were drooping feathers, paper roses, crystal dangles, and leather coiled into horns, each item displayed on green glass heads that stood in front of a large, broken mirror. He had settled on wearing a white tank-top tucked into bland gray Dockers, but when he stood himself next to all his treasures, he felt unfinished. He clipped on black suspenders and looked at himself again. That was better, almost a compromise. A fedora, a cane, and a swirl of eyeliner would have finished off the look, but he left it alone.

"What do you think?" he asked the mirror, but it did not answer. He looked at the unpainted plaster face casts resting on a nearby shelf; their hollow eyes told him nothing either.

Rafe tucked his little phone into his front left pocket with his wallet and keys. He would call his father from the train. He glanced at the wall, at one of the sketches of costumes he'd done for a postmodern ballet production of *Hamlet*. An award hung beside it. This sketch was of a faceless woman in a white gown appliqued with leaves and berries. He remembered how dancers had held the girl up while others pulled on the red ribbons he had had hidden in her sleeves. Yards and yards of red ribbon had come from her wrists. The stage had been swathed in red. The dancers had been covered in red. The whole world had become one dripping gash of ribbon.

The train ride was dull. He felt guilty that the green landscapes that blurred outside the window did not stir him. He only loved leaves if they were crafted from velvet.

Rafael's father waited at the station in the same old blue truck he'd had since before Rafe had left Jersey for good. Each trip his father would ask him careful questions about his job, the city, Rafe's apartment. Certain assumptions were made. His father would tell him about some cousin getting into trouble, or lately, about how Mary was going to leave Marco. Rafe's father was sure Marco was messing around with another girl. With Marco, there was always another girl.

Rafe leaned back in the passenger seat, feeling the heat of

the sun wash away the last of the goose bumps on his arms. He had forgotten how cold the air conditioning was on the train. His father's skin, sun-darkened to deep mahogany, made his own seem sickly pale. A string-tied box of crystallized ginger pastries sat at his feet. He always brought something for his parents: a bottle of wine, a tarte tatin, a jar of truffle oil from Balducci's. Something to remind him that his ticket was round-trip, bought and paid for.

"Mary's getting a divorce," Rafe's father said once he'd pulled out of the parking lot. "She's been staying in your old room. I had to move your sewing stuff."

"Does Marco know yet?" Rafe had already heard about the divorce; his sister had called him a week ago at three in the morning from Cherry Hill, asking for money so she and her son Victor could take a bus home. She had talked in heaving breaths and he'd guessed she'd been crying. He had wired the money to her from the corner store where he often went for green tea ice cream. Now, this detail stuck in his throat.

"He sure does. He wants to see his son. I told him if he comes around the house again, your cousin's gonna break probation but he's also gonna break that loco sonofabitch's neck."

No one, of course, thought that spindly Rafe was going to break Marco's neck.

The truck passed people dragging lawn chairs into their front yards for a better view of the coming fireworks. Although it was still many hours until dark, neighbors milled around, drinking lemonade and beer. In the back of the Santiago house, smoke pillared up from the grill where cousin Gabriel scorched hamburger patties smothered in hot sauce. Mary lay on the blue couch in front of the TV, an ice mask covering her eyes. Rafael walked by as quietly as he could. The house was dark and the radio was turned way down. For once, his greeting was subdued. Only his nephew, Victor, a sparkler twirling in his hand, seemed oblivious to the somber mood.

They ate watermelon so cold that it was better than drinking water; hot dogs and hamburgers off the grill with more hot sauce and tomatoes; rice and beans; corn salad; and ice cream. They drank beer and instant iced tea and the decent tequila that Gabriel had brought. Mary joined them halfway through the meal and Rafe was only half-surprised to see the blue and yellow bruise darkening her jaw. Mostly, he was surprised how much her face, angry and suspicious of pity, reminded him of Lyle.

When Rafe and Lyle were thirteen, they had been best friends. Lyle had lived across town with his grandparents and three sisters in a house far too small for all of them. His grandmother told the kids terrible stories to keep them from going near the river that ran through the woods behind their yard. There was the one about phooka, who appeared like a goat with sulfurous yellow eyes and great curling horns and who shat on the blackberries on the first of November. There was the kelpie that swam in the river and wanted to carry off Lyle and his sisters to drown and devour. And there were the trooping faeries that would steal them all away to their underground hills for a hundred years.

Lyle and Rafe snuck out to the woods anyway. They would stretch out on an old, bug-infested mattress and "practice" sex.

Lyle had forbidden certain conversations. There were never to be conversations about the practicing, no conversations about the bruises on his back and arms, and no conversations about his grandfather, ever, at all. Rafe thought about that, about all the conversations he had learned not to have, all the conversations he was still avoiding.

As fireworks lit up the black sky, Rafe listened to his sister fight with Marco on the phone. He must have been accusing her about getting the money from a lover because he heard his name said over and over. "Rafael sent it," she shouted. "My fucking brother sent it." Finally, she screamed that if he didn't stop threatening her she was going to call the police. She said her cousin was a cop. And it was true; Teo Santiago was a cop. But Teo was also in jail.

When she got off the phone, Rafe said nothing. He didn't want her to think he'd overheard.

She came over anyway. "Thanks for everything, you know? The money and all."

He looked up at her and couldn't help but touch the side of her face with the bruise. She looked at the ground but he could see that her eyes had grown wet.

"You're gonna be okay," he said. "You're gonna be happier."

"I know," she said. One of the tears tumbled from her eye and shattered across the toe of his expensive leather shoe, tiny fragments sparkling with reflected light. "I didn't want you to hear all this shit. Your life is always so together."

"Not really," he said, smiling. Mary had seen his apartment only once, when she and Marco had brought Victor up to see the Lion King. Rafe had sent her tickets; they were hard to get so he thought that she might want them. They hadn't stayed long in his apartment; the costumes that hung on the walls had frightened Victor.

She smiled too. "Have you ever had a boyfriend this bad?"

Her words hung in the air a moment. It was the first time any of them had ventured a guess. "Worse," he said, "and girlfriends, too. I have terrible taste."

Mary sat down next to him on the bench. "Girlfriends, too?"

He nodded and lifted a glass of iced tea to his mouth. "When you don't know what you're searching for," he said, "you have to look absolutely everywhere."

The summer that they were fourteen, a guy had gone down on Rafe in one of the public showers at the beach and he gloried in the fact that for the first time he had a story of almost endless interest to Lyle. It was the summer that they almost ran away.

"I saw grandma's faeries," Lyle had said the week before they were supposed to go. He told Rafe plainly, like he'd spotted a robin outside the window.

"How do you know?" Rafe had been making a list of things they needed to bring. The pen in his hand had stopped writing in the middle of spelling "colored pencils." For a moment, all Rafe felt was resentment that his blowjob story had been trumped.

"They were just the way she said they'd be. Dancing in a circle and they glowed a little, like their skin could reflect the moonlight. One of them looked at me and her face was as beautiful as the stars."

Rafe scowled. "I want to see them too."

"Before we get on the train we'll go down to where I saw them dancing."

Rafe added "peanut butter" to his list. It was the same list he was double checking six days later, when Lyle's grandmother called. Lyle was dead. He had slit his wrists in a tub of warm water the night before they were supposed to leave for forever.

Rafe had stumbled to the viewing, cut off a lock of Lyle's blond hair right in front of his pissed-off family, stumbled to the funeral, slept stretched out on the freshly filled grave. It hadn't made sense. He wouldn't accept it. He wouldn't go home.

Rafe took out his wallet and unfolded the train schedule from the billfold. He had a little time. He was always careful not to miss the last train. He looked at the small onyx and silver ring on his pinkie. It had a secret compartment inside, so well hidden that you could barely see the hinge. When Lyle had given it to him, Rafe's fingers had been so slender that it had fit on his ring finger as easily as the curl of Lyle's hair fit inside of it.

As Rafe rose to kiss his mother and warn his father that he would have to be leaving, Mary thrust open the screen door so hard it banged against the plastic trashcan behind it.

"Where's Victor? Is he inside with you? He's supposed to be in bed."

Rafe shook his head. His mother immediately put down the plate she was drying and walked through the house, still holding the dishrag and calling Victor's name. Mary showed them how his bed was stuffed with pillows that formed a small boy-shape under the blankets.

Mary stared at Rafe as though he was hiding her son from her. "He's not here. He's gone."

"Maybe he snuck out to see some friends," Rafe said, but it didn't seem right. Victor was only ten.

"Marco couldn't have come here without us seeing him," Rafe's father protested.

"He's *gone,*" Mary repeated, as though that explained everything. She slumped down in one of the kitchen chairs and covered her face with her hands. "You don't know what he might do to that kid. O God. *Madre de Dios.*"

Rafe's mother came back in the room and punched numbers into the phone. There was no answer at Marco's apartment. She dialed the cousins next. They had mixed opinions on what to do. They had kids of their own and some thought that Mary didn't have the right to take Victor away from his father. Soon everyone in the kitchen was shouting.

Rafe got up and went to the window, looking out into the dark backyard. Kids made up their own games and wound up straying farther than they meant to.

"Victor!" he called, walking across the lawn. "Victor!"

But he wasn't there, and when Rafe walked out to the street, he could not find the boy along the hot asphalt length. Although it was night, the sky was bright with a full moon and clouds enough to reflect the city lights.

A car slowed as it came down the street. It sped away once it was past the house and Rafe let out the breath he didn't even realize that he had held. His brother-in-law had never seemed crazy to him, just bored and maybe a little resentful that he had a wife and a kid. But then, Lyle's grandfather had seemed normal, too.

Rafe thought about the train schedule in his pocket and the

unfinished sketches on his desk. It was getting late. The last train would be along soon and if he wasn't there to meet it, he would have to spend the night with his memories. There was nothing he could do here. In the city, he could call around and find her the number of a good lawyer—a lawyer that Marco couldn't afford. That was the best thing, he thought. But he'd turned despite himself, his shoes clicking like beetles on the pavement.

His oldest cousin had come out to talk to him in the graveyard the night after Lyle's funeral. It had clearly creeped Teo to find his little cousin sleeping in the cemetery, but Rafael's mother had sent him to bring Rafael home and Teo was used to the obligations of family.

"He's gone." Teo had squatted down in his blue policeman uniform. He sounded a little impatient and very awkward.

"The faeries took him," Rafe had said. "They stole him away to Faerieland and left something else in his place."

"Then he's still not in this graveyard." Teo had pulled on Rafe's arm and Rafe had finally stood.

"If I hadn't touched him," Rafe had said, so softly that maybe Teo didn't hear.

It didn't matter. Even if Teo had heard, he would have pretended he hadn't.

Rafe walked out of the house, hearing the distant fireworks and twirling his father's keys around his first finger. He hadn't taken the truck without permission in years.

The stick and clutch were hard to time and the engine grunted and groaned, but when he made it to the highway, he flicked on the radio and stayed in fifth gear the whole way to Cherry Hill. Marco's house was easy to find. The lights were on in every room and the blue flicker of the television lit up the front steps.

Rafe parked around a corner and walked up to the window of the guest bedroom. When he was thirteen, he had snuck into Lyle's house lots of times. Lyle had slept on a pullout mattress in the living room because his sisters shared the second bedroom. The trick was waiting until the television was off and everyone else was in bed. Rafe excelled at waiting.

When the house finally went silent and dark, Rafe pushed the window. It was unlocked. He slid it up as far as he could and pulled himself inside.

Victor turned over sleepily and opened his eyes. They went wide.

Rafe froze and waited for him to scream, but his nephew didn't move.

"It's your uncle," Rafe said softly. "From the Lion King. From New York." He sat down on the carpet. Someone had once told him that being lower was less threatening.

Victor didn't speak.

"Your mom sent me to pick you up."

The mention of his mother seemed to give him the courage to say: "Why didn't you come to the door?"

"Your dad would kick my ass," Rafe said. "I'm not crazy."

Victor half-smiled.

"I could drive you back," Rafe said. He took his cell phone

out of his pocket and put it on the bed by Victor. "You can call your mom and she'll tell you I'm okay."

"Are you going to make a pretend me like Daddy did?" Victor asked.

The words echoed for a long moment before Rafe remembered to shake his head.

On the drive back, Rafe told Victor a story that his mother had told him and Mary when they were little, about a king who fed a louse so well on royal blood that it swelled up so large that it no longer fit in the palace. The king had the louse slaughtered and its hide tanned to make a coat for his daughter, the princess, and told all her suitors that they had to guess what kind of skin she wore before their proposal could be accepted.

Victor liked the part of the story where Rafe pretended to hop like a flea and bite his nephew. Rafe liked all fairy tales with tailors in them.

"Come inside," his mother said. "You should have told us you were going to take the car. I needed to go to the store and get some—"

She stopped, seeing Victor behind Rafael.

Rafe's father stood up from the couch as they came in. Rafe tossed the keys and his father caught them.

"Tough guy." His father grinned. "I hope you hit him."

"Are you kidding? And hurt this delicate hand?" Rafe asked, holding it up for inspection.

He was surprised by his father's laugh.

For the first time in almost fifteen years, Rafe spent the night.

Stretching out on the lumpy couch, he turned the onyx ring again and again on his finger.

Then, for the first time in more than ten years, he thumbed open the hidden compartment, ready to see Lyle's golden hair. Crumbled leaves fell onto his chest instead.

Leaves. Not hair. Hair lasted; it should be there. Victorian mourning ornaments braided with the hair of the long-dead survived decades. Rafe had seen such a brooch on the scarf of a well-known playwright. The hair was dulled by time, perhaps, but it had hardly turned to leaves.

He thought of the lump of bedclothes that had looked like Victor at first glance. A "pretend me," Victor had said. But Lyle's corpse wasn't pretend. He had seen it. He had cut off a lock of its hair.

Rafe ran his fingers through the crushed leaves on his chest.

Hope swelled inside of him, despite the senselessness of it. He didn't like to think about Faerieland lurking just over a hill or beneath a shallow river, as distant as a memory. But if he could believe that he could pass unscathed from the world of the city into the world of the suburban ghetto and back again, then couldn't he go further? Why couldn't he cross into the world of shining people with faces like stars who were the root of all his costumes?

Marco had stolen Victor; but Rafe had stolen Victor back. Until that moment, Rafe hadn't considered he could steal Lyle back from Faeryland.

Rafe kicked off the afghan.

At the entrance to the woods, Rafe stopped and lit a cigarette. His feet knew the way to the river by heart.

The mattress was filthier than he remembered, smeared with dirt and damp with dew. He sat, unthinking, and whispered Lyle's name.

"I went to New York, just like we planned," Rafe said, his hand stroking over the blades of grass as though they were hairs on a pelt. "I got a job in a theatrical rental place, full of these antiqued candelabras and musty old velvet curtains. Now I make stage clothes. I don't ever have to come back here again."

He rested his head against the mattress, inhaled mold and leaves and earth. His face felt heavy, as though already sore with tears. "Do you remember Mary? Her husband hits her. I bet he hits my nephew, too." His eyes were wet with unexpected tears. The guilt that twisted his gut was as fresh and raw as it had been the day Lyle died. "I never knew why you did it. Why you had to die instead of come away with me."

"Lyle," he sighed, and his voice trailed off. He wasn't sure what he'd been about to say. "I just wish you were here, Lyle. I wish you were here to talk to."

Rafe pressed his mouth to the mattress and closed his eyes for a moment before he rose and brushed the dirt off his slacks.

He would just ask Mary what happened with Marco. If Victor was all right. If they wanted to live with him for a while. He would tell his parents that he slept with men. There would be no more secrets, no more assumptions. There was nothing he could do for Lyle now, but there was still something he could do for his nephew.

It was then he saw the lights, springing up from nothing, like matches catching in the dark.

There, in the woods, faeries danced in a circle. They were bright and seemed almost weightless, hair flying behind them like smoke behind a sparkler. Among them, Rafe thought he saw Lyle, looking no older than he did in Rafe's memory, so absorbed in dancing that he did not hear Rafe gasp or shout. He started forward, hand outstretched. At the center of the circle, a woman in a gown of green smiled a cold and terrible smile before the whole company disappeared.

Rafe felt his heart beat hard against his chest. He was frightened as he had not been at fourteen, when magical things seemed like they could be ordinary and ordinary things were almost magical.

On the way home, Rafe thought of all the other fairy tales he knew about tailors. He thought of the faery woman's plain green gown and about desire. When he got to the house, he pulled his sewing machine out of the closet and set it up on the kitchen table. Then he began to rummage through all the cloth and trims, beads and fringe. He found crushed panne velvet that looked like liquid gold and sewed it into a frockcoat studded with bright buttons and appliquéd with blue flames that lapped up the sleeves. It was one of the most beautiful things he had ever made. He fell asleep cradling it and woke to his mother setting a cup of espresso mixed with condensed milk in front of him. He drank the coffee in one slug.

It was easy to make a few phone calls and a few promises, change around meetings and explain to his bewildered parents that he needed to work from their kitchen for a day or two. Of course, Clio would feed his cats. Of course, Joshua understood that Rafe was working through a design problem. Of course, the presentation could be rescheduled for the following Friday. Of course. Of course.

His mother patted his shoulder. "You work too hard."

He nodded, because it was easier than telling her he wasn't really working.

"But you make beautiful things. You sew like your great-grandmother. I told you how people came from miles around to get their wedding dresses made by her."

"You told me." He smiled up at her and thought of all the gifts he had brought at the holidays—cashmere gloves and leather coats and bottles of perfume. He had never sewn a single thing for her. Making gifts had seemed cheap, like he was giving her a child's misshapen vase or a card colored with crayons. But the elegant, meaningless presents he had sent were cold, revealing nothing about him and even less about her. Imagining her in a silk dress the color of papayas—one he might sew himself—filled him with shame.

He slept most of the day in the shadowed dark of his parents' bed with the shades drawn and the door closed. The buzz of cartoons in the background and the smell of cooking oil made him feel like a small child again. When he woke it was dark outside. His clothes had been cleaned and were folded at the foot of the bed. He put the golden coat on over them and walked to the river.

There, he smoked cigarette after cigarette, dropping the filters into the water, listening for the hiss as the river smothered the flame and drowned the paper. Finally, the faeries came, dancing their endless dance, with the cold faery woman sitting in the middle.

The woman saw him and walked through the circle. Her eyes were green as moss and, as she got close, he saw that her hair flowed behind her as though she were swimming through water or like ribbons whipped in a fierce wind. Where she stepped, tiny flowers bloomed.

"Your coat is beautiful. It glows like the sun," the faery said, reaching out to touch the fabric.

"I would give it to you," said Rafe. "Just let me have Lyle."

A smile twisted her mouth. "I will let you spend tonight with him. If he remembers you, he is free to go. Will that price suit?"

Rafe nodded and removed the coat.

The faery woman caught Lyle's hand as he spun past, pulling him out of the dance. He was laughing, still, as his bare feet touched the moss outside the circle and he aged. His chest grew broader, he became taller, his hair lengthened, and fine lines appeared around his mouth and eyes. He was no longer a teenager.

"Leaving us, even for a time, has a price," the faery woman said. Standing on her toes, she bent Lyle's head to her lips. His eyelids drooped and she steered him to the moldering mattress. He never even looked in Rafe's direction; he just sank down into sleep.

"Lyle," Rafe said, dropping down beside him, smoothing the tangle of hair back from his face. There were braids in it that knotted up with twigs and leaves and cords of thorny vines. A smudge of dirt highlighted one cheekbone. Leaves blew over him, but he did not stir.

"Lyle," Rafe said again. Rafe was reminded of how Lyle's body had lain in the casket at the funeral, of how Lyle's skin had been pale and bluish as skim milk and smelled faintly of chemicals, of how his fingers were threaded together across his chest so tightly that when Rafe tried to take his hand, it was stiff as a mannequin's. Even now, the memory of that other, dead Lyle seemed more real than the one that slept beside him like a cursed prince in a fairy tale.

"Please wake up," Rafe said. "Please. Wake up and tell me this is real."

Lyle did not stir. Beneath the lids, his eyes moved as if he saw another landscape.

Rafe shook him and then struck him, hard, across the face. "Get up," he shouted. He tugged on Lyle's arm and Lyle's body rolled toward him.

Standing, he tried to lift Lyle, but he was used to only the weight of bolts of cloth. He settled for dragging him toward the street where Rafe could flag down a car or call for help. He pulled with both his hands, staining Lyle's shirt and face with grass, and scratching his side on a fallen branch. Rafe dropped his hand and bent over him in the quiet dark.

"It's too far," Rafe said. "Far too far."

He stretched out beside Lyle, pillowing his friend's head against his chest and resting on his own arm.

When Rafe woke, Lyle was no longer beside him, but the faery woman was there. She wore the coat of fire, and, in the light of the newly risen sun, she shone so brightly that Rafe had to shade his eyes with his hand. She laughed and her laugh sounded like ice cracking on a frozen lake.

"You cheated me," Rafe said. "You made him sleep."

"He heard you in his dreams," said the faery woman. "He preferred to remain dreaming."

Rafe stood and brushed off his pants, but his jaw clenched so tightly that his teeth hurt.

"Come with me," the faery said. "Join the dance. You are only jealous that you were left behind. Let that go. You can be forever young and you can make beautiful costumes forevermore. We will appreciate them as no mortal does and we will adore you."

Rafe inhaled the leaf-mold and earth smells. Where Lyle had rested, a golden hair remained. He thought of his mother and sister and father. He thought of Victor and the wall of masks waiting for him at home. He thought of the frantic director who had begged him for costumes in two weeks for a play she wrote herself. Rafe wound the hair around his finger so tightly that it striped his skin white and red. "No," he told her.

His mother was sitting in her robe in the kitchen. She got up when Rafe came in.

"Where are you going? You are like a possessed man." She touched his hand and her skin felt so hot that he pulled back in surprise.

"You're freezing! You have been at his grave."

It was easier for Rafe to nod than explain.

"There is a story about a woman who mourned too long and the spectre of her lover rose up and dragged her down into death with him."

He nodded again, thinking of the faery woman, of being dragged into the dance, of Lyle sleeping like death.

She sighed exaggeratedly and made him a coffee. Rafe had already set up the sewing machine by the time she put the mug beside him.

That day he made a coat of silver silk, pleated at the hips and embroidered with a tangle of thorny branches and lapels of downy white fur. He knew it was one of the most beautiful things he had ever made.

"Who are you sewing that for?" Mary asked when she came in. "It's gorgeous."

He rubbed his eyes and gave her a tired smile. "It's supposed to be the payment a mortal tailor used to win back a lover from Faeryland."

"I haven't heard of that story," his sister said. "Will it be a musical?"

"I don't know yet," said Rafe. "I don't think the cast can sing."

His mother frowned and called Mary over to chop up a summer squash.

"I want you and Victor to come live with me," Rafe said as his sister turned away from him.

"Your place is too small," Rafe's mother told him.

She had never seen his apartment. "We could move, then. Go to Queens. Brooklyn."

"You won't want a little boy running around. And Mary has

the cousins here. She should stay with us. Besides, the city is dangerous."

"Marco is dangerous," Rafe said, voice rising. "Why don't you let Mary make up her own mind?"

Rafe's mother muttered under her breath as she chopped, Rafe sighed and bit his tongue and Mary gave him a sisterly roll of the eyes. It occurred to him that that had been the most normal conversation he had had with his mother in years.

All day Rafe worked on the sleeves of the garment and that night he, wearing the silvery coat, went back to the woods and the river.

The dancers were there as before and when Rafe got close, the faery woman left the circle of dancers.

"Your coat is as lovely as the moon. Will you agree to the same terms?"

Rafe thought of objecting, but he also thought of the faery woman's kiss. Maybe he could change the course of events. It would be better if he caught her off-guard. He shouldered off his coat. "I agree."

As before, the faery woman pulled Lyle from the dance.

"Lyle!" Rafe said, starting toward him before the faery could touch his brow with her lips.

Lyle turned to him and his lips parted as though he were searching for a name to go with a distant memory, as if Lyle didn't recall him after all.

The faery woman kissed him then, and Lyle staggered drowsily to the mattress. His drooping eyelashes nearly hid the gaze he gave Rafe. His mouth moved, but no sound escaped him and then he subsided into sleep.

That night Rafe tried a different way of rousing Lyle. He pressed his mouth to Lyle's slack lips, to his forehead as the faery woman had done. He kissed the hollow of Lyle's throat, where the beat of his heart thrummed against his skin. He ran his hands over Lyle's chest, feeling the way it rose and fell with a sigh. He touched his lips to the smooth, unscarred expanse of Lyle's wrists. Again and again, he kissed Lyle, but it was as terrible as kissing a corpse.

Before he slept, Rafe took the onyx and silver ring off his own pinkie, pulled out a strand of black hair from his own head and coiled it inside the hollow of the poison ring. Then he pushed the ring onto Lyle's pinkie.

"Remember me. Please remember me," Rafe said. "I can't remember myself unless you remember me."

But Lyle did not stir and Rafe woke alone on the mattress. He made his way home in the thin light of dawn.

That day he sewed a coat from velvet as black as the night sky. He stiched tiny black crystals onto it and embroidered it with black roses, thicker at the hem and then thinning as they climbed. At the cuffs and neck, ripped ruffles of thin smoky purples and deep reds reminded him of sunsets. Across the back, he sewed on silver beads for stars. Stars like the faery woman's eyes. It was the most beautiful thing Rafael had ever created. He knew he would never make its equal.

That night he donned the coat and walked to the woods.

The faery woman was waiting for him. She sucked in her breath at the sight of the magnificent coat.

"I must have it," she said. "You shall have him as before."

Rafael nodded. Tonight if he could not rouse Lyle, he would

have to say goodbye. Perhaps this was the life Lyle had chosen—a life of dancing and youth and painless memory—and he was wrong to try and take him away from it. But he wanted to spend one more night beside Lyle.

She brought Lyle to him and he knelt on the mattress. The faerie woman bent to kiss his forehead, but at the last moment, Lyle turned his head and the kiss fell on his hair.

Scowling, she rose.

Lyle blinked as though awakening from a long sleep. Then, touching the onyx ring on his finger, he turned toward Rafe and smiled tentatively.

"Lyle?" Rafe asked. "Do you remember me?"

"Rafael?" Lyle asked. He reached a hand toward Rafe's face, fingers skimming just above the skin. Rafe leaned into the heat, butting his head against Lyle's hand and sighing. Time seemed to flow backwards and he felt like he was fourteen again and in love.

"Come, Lyle," said the faery woman sharply.

Lyle rose stiffly, his fingers ruffling Rafe's hair.

"Wait," Rafe said. "He knows who I am. You said he would be free."

"He's as free to come with me as he is to go with you," she said.

Lyle looked down at Rafe. "I dreamed that we went to New York and that we performed in a circus. I danced with the bears and you trained fleas to jump through the eyes of needles."

"I trained fleas?"

"In my dream. You were famous for it." His smile was tentative, uncertain. Maybe he realized that it didn't sound like a great career.

Rafe thought of the story he had told Victor about the princess in her louse-skin coat, about locks of hair and all the things he had managed through the eyes of needles.

The faery woman turned away from them with a scowl, walking back to the fading circle of dancers, becoming insubstantial as smoke.

"It didn't go quite like that." Rafe stood and held out his hand. "I'll tell you what really happened."

Lyle clasped Rafe's fingers in a bruising grip, but his smile was wide and his eyes were bright as stars. "Don't leave anything out."

Paper Cuts Scissors

000 – Generalities

WHEN JUSTIN STARTED GRADUATE school in library science, he tried to sit next to the older women who now needed a degree as media specialists to keep the same job they'd done for years. He avoided the hipster girls, fresh from undergrad, wearing black turtlenecks with silver jewelry molded in menacing shapes and planning careers in public libraries. Those girls seemed as dangerous as books that unexpectedly killed their protagonists.

He wasn't used to being around people anymore. He fidgeted with his freshly cut hair and ran shaking fingers over the razor burn on his pale skin. He didn't meet anyone's eyes as he dutifully learned about new user interfaces and how to conduct a reference interview. He wrote papers with pages of citations. He read pile after pile of genre novels to understand what people saw in inspirational romance or forensic mysteries, but he was careful to read the ends before the beginnings. He told himself that he could hold it together.

At night, when all his reading was done and he'd printed

all the papers he needed for the next day, he tried not to open Linda's book.

He'd read it so many times that he should know it by heart, but the words kept changing. She was always in danger. She'd nearly got run over by a train and frozen on a long march to Moscow while Justin had sat on his parent's pullout couch in the den and forgotten to eat. While his hair had grown long and his fingernails jagged. Until his friends had stopped coming over. Until he'd remembered the one thing he could do to get her out.

One afternoon, Justin checked the notice board and saw a sign:

> Looking for library student to organize private collection: 555-2164. $10/hour.

His heart sped. Finally. It had to be. He punched the number into his cell phone and a man answered.

"Please," Justin said. He had practiced a convincing speech, but he couldn't remember a word of it. His voice shook. "I need this job. I'm very dedicated, very conscientio—"

"You're hired," said the man.

Relief made him lightheaded. He sagged against the painted cinderblock wall of the hallway.

After, in Classification Theory, Sarah Peet turned half around in her chair. Her earrings swung like daggers. "Rock, paper, scissors for who buys coffee at the break."

"Coffee?" His voice came out louder than he'd intended.

"From the vending machine," she said and made a fist.

One. Two. Three. Rock breaks scissors. Justin lost.

"I take it black," said Sarah.

100 – Philosophy and Psychology

The private collection that Justin was supposed to organize was located in the basement of a large Victorian house outside New Brunswick. He drove there in his beat-up Altima and parked in the driveway. He didn't see another car and wondered if Mr. Sandlin—the man he was sure he'd spoken with on the phone—had forgotten that he was coming. According to his watch, it was quarter to seven in the evening. He was fifteen minutes early.

When Justin knocked on the door, he was met by a gentleman in a waistcoat. He had a slight paunch and long hair tied back in a ponytail.

"Excellent," the man said. "Eager. I'm Sandlin."

"Justin," said Justin. He hoped his palms weren't sweating.

"Each year I hire a new library student—you'll pick up where the last one left off. Dewey decimal. No Library of Congress, got it?"

"I understand perfectly," Justin said.

Sandlin led Justin through a house shrouded in white sheeting, down a dusty staircase to a cavernous basement. Masses of bookshelves formed a maze beneath swaying chandeliers. Justin sucked in his breath.

"There's a desk somewhere that way," Sandlin said. "A computer. Some books still in boxes. I used to run a bookshop, but I found that I wasn't suited for it. I didn't like when people bought things. I like to have all my books with me."

It was a vast, amazing collection. Justin could feel his pulse speed and a smile creep onto his face.

"Best to get started," said Sandlin, turning and walking back up the stairs. "You have to leave before midnight. I have guests."

Justin couldn't imagine that there'd been many visitors entering through the front door, considering how thick the dust was upstairs. The wooden planks under his feet, however, were swept clean.

Sandlin stopped at the landing, gesturing grandly as he called down. "It is my belief that books are living things."

That sent a shiver up Justin's spine as he thought of Linda.

"And as living things, they need to be protected." Sandlin walked the rest of the way up the stairs.

Justin rubbed his arms and bit back what he wanted to say. It was readers that needed to be protected, he thought. Books were something that happened to readers. Readers were the victims of books.

He'd considered this a lot at the bookstore, once Linda was gone and before he'd lost the job altogether. Grim-faced women would come in, dressed sensibly, pleading for a sequel like they were pleading for a lover's life. Children would sit on the rug and cry inconsolably over picture books where rabbits lost their mothers.

The desk—when he found it—was ordinary, gray metal rusted at the corners and the PC sitting on top was old enough that it had a floppy drive. The keyboard felt sticky under his fingers. Justin opened his backpack and looked in at Linda's book; when packing the night before, he found that he couldn't bring himself to leave it behind.

200 – Religion

Justin had always opened new books with a sense of dread, but no dread could compare with opening Linda's book. Sometimes the *militsiya* were arresting a member of her new family, or she was swallowing priceless rubies so that she could smuggle them out of Russia. Occasionally she was in love. Or drinking strong tea out of a samovar. Or dancing.

He remembered her with ink-stained fingers and a messy apartment full of paperbacks. He'd lived there with her when they both worked in the bookstore. She was allergic to cats, but she couldn't resist petting the stray that the owner kept and her nose was always red from sneezing. She made spaghetti with olives when she was depressed.

He remembered the way they'd curled up together on the futon and read to one another. He remembered his laughing confession that he opened new books with a sense of dread akin to jumping off a cliff with a bungee on. He knew he probably wouldn't hit the rocks, but he was never really sure. Linda didn't understand. She read fearlessly, without care for how things turned out.

Things, she said, could always be changed.

She told him that she knew how to fold stuff up and put it in books. *In* the books, inside the stories themselves. She'd proven it to him. She put a single playing card into a paperback edition of *Robin Hood.* The Ace of Spades. Little John had found it. He'd become convinced it was a sign that they would be defeated by the Sheriff of Nottingham and hanged himself. The Merry Men were less merry after they found his body. Justin had looked at other editions of *Robin Hood,* but they were unchanged.

After that, he'd believed her. He'd wanted her to alter other books—like fix *Macbeth* so that no one died. She said that *Macbeth* was unlucky enough without her tampering.

They'd fought a lot in their third year together. Linda had heard that there was a man named Mr. Sandlin who could take things out of books as well as putting them in. She wanted them to give up the lease on their apartment and their jobs at the bookstore. She wanted them to enroll in library school. Early one morning, after fighting all night—a fight that had started out about moving and wound up about every hateful thing they'd ever thought about one another—she folded herself up and put herself into a fat Russian novel.

"Ohgodohgodohgod," Justin had said. "Please. No. Please. Oh God. Please." He'd opened the cover to see an illustration of her in pen and ink, sitting in a group of unsmiling characters.

After that, he couldn't tell her that he was sorry or that her bolshie-sympathizing uncle was going to expose her in the next chapter or that she was going to regret leaving him now that she was stuck in an ice storm with only a mink cloak and muff to protect her. He was just a reader and readers can't do anything to make the story stop—except close the book.

300 – *Social Sciences*

The next time that Sandlin opened the door, he was dressed less impressively, in pajamas with blue stripes. He greeted Justin with a huge yawn.

"Am I early?" Justin asked, although he knew he wasn't.

Sandlin shook his head and waved Justin in. "Time I got up anyway."

"Right. I'll be downstairs," said Justin as Sandlin dumped out the coffeepot and filled it with water from the tap.

The collection, which had looked so grand at first sight, was, on closer inspection, quite odd. None of the books seemed to be first editions. Many were not even hardcover. Tattered paperbacks nestled up against reprinted hardcover editions of classics with their spines cracked. Some books even appeared to be galleys from publishers, marked, "FOR REVIEW PURPOSES ONLY—NOT FOR RESALE."

Most of the books were easy to classify. They were almost all 800s, mostly 810s or 820s.

He glanced at the backs of their covers and the copyright pages and then typed their titles into the database. On the spines of each, he taped a label printed in marker.

After he finished a dozen, Justin decided that he should start shelving. He lifted the stack, inhaling book dust, and headed into the aisles.

The problem with everything being in the 800s is that the markers on the ends of the shelves blurred together. Justin took a few turns and then wasn't sure he knew where he was going or where he could find the places for the books in his arms.

"Sandlin?" he called, but although his voice echoed in the vast room, he doubted it was loud enough to carry all the way upstairs.

He turned again. A plastic drink stirrer rested on the floor. Bending to pick it up, he felt panic rise. Where was he? He'd thought he was retracing his steps.

By the time he found his way back to the desk, he felt a faintly ridiculous but almost overwhelming sense of relief.

Sarah leaned back in her seat and sat a roll of twine in front of him.

"I heard you got the Sandlin job," Sarah said. "My friend used to work there, said it was like a maze. This is his Theseus trick."

"That's smart," Justin said, thinking of Theseus picking his way through the Minotaur's lair, unwinding Ariadne's string behind him. Thinking of how his heart had pounded when he was lost in the stacks. It wasn't just smart, it was *clever,* even classical. He wished he'd thought of it.

"Rock, paper, scissors to see if I can come with you."

"No way," Justin said. "I could lose my job."

"My friend said some other stuff—about what happens after midnight. Come on. If you win, I'll tell you everything I know. If I win, I get to come."

"Fine." Justin scowled, but Sarah didn't seem cowed. She raised a brow studded with tiny silver bars.

Rock. Paper. Scissors. Her rock smashed his scissors.

"Best two out of three," Justin said, but he knew he was already defeated.

"Tomorrow night," said Sarah, with a smile that he couldn't interpret. In fact, the more he thought about it, the less he knew about why she'd started talking to him at all.

400 – *Language*

That night, Justin tucked the string and Linda's book into his backpack and drove to Sandlin's house. He worked his way through cataloging an entire box of books, when, on impulse, he flipped a thin volume open.

The spine of the book read *Pride and Prejudice* so Justin was surprised to find Indiana Jones in the text. Apparently, he'd been sleeping his way through all the Jane Austen books and had seduced both Kitty and Lydia Bennett. Justin discovered this fact when Eleanor Tilney from *Northanger Abbey* showed up to confront Indy with his illegitimate child.

He looked at the page and read it twice just to be sure:

To Catherine and Lydia, neither Miss Tilney nor her claims were in any degree interesting. It was next to impossible that Miss Tilney had told the truth, and although it was now some weeks since they had received pleasure from the society of Mr. Jones, they had every confidence in him. As for their mother, she was weathering the blow with a degree of composure which astonished her husband and daughters.

He closed the book, set it back on the shelf, and opened another. *Peter Pan.* In it, Sherlock Holmes deduced that Tinkerbell had poisoned

Wendy while Watson complained to the mermaids that no one understood his torrid romance with one of the shepherdesses from a poem. Wendy's ghost flitted around quoting lines from *Macbeth*. Peter wasn't in the book at all. He'd left to be a valet to Lord Rochester in a play of which no one had ever heard.

Justin shut *Peter Pan* so quickly that one of the pages cut a thin line in his index finger. He stuck his bleeding finger in his mouth and tasted ink and sweat. It made him feel vaguely nauseous.

500 – Natural Sciences & Mathematics

Scrambling over to his backpack, Justin started unrolling the string. It dragged across the floors, through the aisles as he wound his way though the maze of shelves. At first, it was just books, but as he moved deeper into the stacks, he discovered a statue of a black-haired man in a long blue robe and eyes that glittered like they were set with glass, a velvet fainting couch, and a forgotten collection of champagne flutes containing the dregs of a greenish liquid beside a single jet button.

He glanced at the shelves, thinking of Sandlin's pajamas and Sarah's words: *My friend said some other stuff—about what happens after midnight.* A party happened here, a party with guests that never disturbed the dust upstairs, that never entered or exited through the front hall.

A party with guests that were already in the house. Guests that were *inside the books.*

He shuddered then laughed a little at himself. This was what he'd been hoping for, after all. Now he had to just count on the fact that Sandlin wouldn't notice one more book.

That night Justin called out his usual farewell to Mr. Sandlin, before sneaking back down the library stairs. He climbed one of the old ladders along the far wall and cracked open a high, thin window. Then he rolled onto the very top of the bookshelf and flattened himself against the wood. Something banged against the glass.

"Wow. We're pretty high up," said Sarah as she slid inside. Her foot knocked a stack of papers and a bookend shaped like a nymph crashed to the floor. "Shit!"

"Careful," whispered Justin. He knew he sounded prissy as soon as it came out of his mouth, but Sarah didn't seem like a very careful person.

"So," she said. She wore a tattered black coat covered in paint stains and a new hoop gleamed in her eyebrow. The skin around it was puffy and red. "Here we are. This is it."

"What's it?"

"This is where Richard hid. My friend. Pretty genius, right? He could see everything from up here. And who ever looks up?" She answered her own question with a nod. "Nobody."

"Did he say what happens now?"

"*The books come to life.*" Her voice was filled with awe, like she was about to take a sacrament from the Holy Church of Literature.

Justin looked at his bag where Linda's Russian novel rested. He had a sudden urge to pitch it out the window. "How do you think that happens? There are so many . . ." He wasn't sure how to end that sentence. Characters? Settings? Books?

A footfall kept him from finding out.

"Shhhh," said Sarah, completely unnecessarily.

Sandlin appeared, walking down the stairs with a crate. Justin crawled forward to see him begin to set up bottles and a cheese platter. He removed red grapes from their plastic-covered package and set them carefully on one end of the tray, then stepped back to look at his arrangement.

He appeared to be satisfied because when he turned around, he made a motion with his hands and a ripple went through the shelves. The books shuddered and then, one by one, the room began to fill with people.

They climbed out of the stacks, brushing themselves off, sometimes hopping from a high place, sometimes crawling out of what seemed like a very cramped low shelf.

Justin looked over at his backpack in time to see women in high-necked dresses and men in uniforms scamper down. He looked for Linda, but from the back, he wasn't sure which one she was. He started to follow, but Sarah grabbed his arm.

"What are you doing?" she hissed. "You said to be careful—remember?"

He leaned over the side, scanning all the faces for Linda's. He tried to remember what she looked like; he kept thinking of lines of description instead. Her hair was "thick chestnut curls like the shining mane of a horse" in the book. He was pretty sure he'd read a passage about her eyes being "amber as the pin at her throat," but he remembered them as brown.

Women with powdered cones of hair and black masks on sticks swept past knights decked out for jousting and comic book heroes in slinky, rubbery suits. A wolf in a top hat and tails conversed with a wizard in a robe of moons and stars as faeries flew over their heads.

He thought he saw Linda near the grapes, whispering behind a fan. He strained to hear what she said, but all he heard were other conversations. Without quite meaning to, he realized what he was hearing.

"Sarah." Justin pointed to a large-shouldered man decked out in lace, with a slim sword at his hip and a small reddish flower in his hands. He was lazily chatting up a skinny, red-headed young woman in jeans and a t-shirt.

"Demmed smart you are," said the man. "Pretty, too. I've been assured my taste is unerring so there's no need to protest."

"Sarah," said Justin. "That's the Scarlet Pimpernel!"

"Oh my god," Sarah whispered back, wriggling closer. "I think you're right. Percy Blakeney. I had such a crush on him."

"I think he's hitting on that girl."

"Isn't that?" She paused. "It can't be . . . but I think the girl is Anne of Green Gables."

Justin squinted. "I never read it."

"I heard her say something about there being no one like him in Avonlea," said Sarah. "What's she doing in jeans? Anne! Anne! Don't do it!"

"Shhh!" Justin said.

"He's married! Marguerite will kick your ass!"

Justin tried to put his hand over her mouth. "You can't just—"

Sarah pulled away, but she seemed a little bit embarrassed. "Chill out. She couldn't hear me anyway. And I wasn't the one who almost climbed down there."

He looked back into the crowd, tamping down both rising panic and chaotic glee. Characters shouldn't be able to meet like this, to mix and converse anachronistically and anarchically in the basement of a house in Jersey. It seemed profane, perverse, and yet it was the perversion itself that tempted him to dangerous joy.

"Okay. Jeesh," said Sarah, mistaking the reason for his silence. "I'm sorry I got carried away—hey, who's that in the gold armor? Standing near. Oh." She stopped. "Is that Wolverine talking to a wolverine? In a dress?"

"Which one's wearing the dress?" Justin asked, but the grin slid off his face when he saw Linda move away from the refreshments. She was talking to a man in a doublet.

Sarah put her hand on his arm. "Who are you staring at? You look really weird."

"That's my girlfriend," said Justin.

"A character in a book is your girlfriend?"

"She put herself there. We had an argument—it's not important. I'm just trying to get her out again."

Sarah stared at him, but her expression said: *I don't believe you. You did something bad to your girlfriend to make her put herself in a book.* Her earrings swung like pendulums, dowsing for guilty secrets. "You knew what was going on when you applied for this job, didn't you?"

"So?" Justin asked. "Oh, you wanted it too, didn't you? I just called first."

"Well, she's out from the book now. You don't look too happy."

Justin scowled and they said little to each other after that. They just rested on their stomachs on the dusty bookshelves and watched the crowd swirl and eddy beneath them, watched Little

Lord Fauntleroy piss in a corner and an albino in armor mutter to the black sword in his hands as he headed for one of the more private and shadowed parts of the library.

And Justin watched as Linda flitted among them, laughing with pleasure.

"Oh, you doth teach the torches to burn bright," the man in the doublet told her.

What a line, Justin thought ruefully. *I hope she knows he's quoting Shakespeare.* Then an unpleasant thought occurred to him. *Who was Linda talking to?*

"Lo, John Galt hath eaten all the salsa," said a knight in green armor adorned with leaves.

"Oh, how awful," said Dolly Alexandrovna from *Anna Karenina.* She smoothed her gown, looking exactly like a painting of her Justin had seen. "I won't forgive him and I can't forgive him. He persists in doing this every night."

Justin wondered why none of them spoke in Russian or French or whatever, but then it occurred to him that all the books were in translation. The logic made him dizzy.

"Who's John Galt?" growled Wolverine around the cigar in his mouth.

Anne of Green Gables danced a waltz with a man that Justin failed to recognize and wasn't going to ask Sarah about. Stephen Daedalus got into a fistfight with Werther. Hamlet shouted at them to stop, yelling, "it is but foolery," but they didn't stop until Werther got hit hard enough that his nose bled.

Justin thought that after being punched, he looked weirdly like the guy on the cover of the Modern Library reprint edition of *Werther,* where his whole face is wet with tears.

"How can I, how can you, be annihilated?" Werther spat. "We exist. What is annihilation? A mere word, an unmeaning sound that fixes no impression on the mind."

Stephen's knuckles looked bruised. "Whatever," he said.

Linda sunk down beside Werther, silky skirts billowing around her, and dabbed at the blood on his face with a handkerchief. What was she doing? It made no sense! She didn't even like Goethe! She'd complained that Werther was a coward and whiny, besides.

Justin started to climb down the bookshelf.

Sandlin shouted something at that moment and then a great gust of wind blew through the library and when it had gone, so had all the party guests.

Gone. Linda was gone. Justin looked out the small window and, sure enough, the sky was beginning to lighten outside. Reaching for his pack, he opened Linda's book and flipped frantically, scanning each page for her name.

Nothing.

Gone.

600 – *Technology (Applied Sciences)*

The next day at the break, Sarah brought a cup of coffee from the machine and set it on the desk in front of him without resorting to rock, paper, or scissors. He still wore the same clothes from the night before and when he looked down at his notebook, all he had written was "faceted classification" with several lines drawn under the words. He had no idea what that meant.

"I should be mad at you," she said, "but you're just too pathetic."

He picked up the coffee and took a sip. He was glad it was warm.

She sat on the edge of his desk. "Okay, so tell me about your girlfriend. What happened?"

"I don't know. We just started fighting. She wanted to meet Sandlin, but I wanted to stay at the bookstore. Then this."

"And by *this*, you mean that instead of locking herself in the bathroom or throwing a vase at you, she put herself in a book and didn't come out."

"Yeah," Justin said, looking at the desk.

"You might seriously consider that that translates to breaking up with you."

He scrubbed his hand over his face. His skin felt rougher than his stubble. "I don't think she knew how to get out." But, as he thought back on it, he couldn't recall reading that she wanted to; characters in Russian novels are big on bemoaning their personal tragedy. It seemed that wouldn't have been left out.

Sarah shrugged. "You said that she wanted to meet Sandlin. You brought her to him. You're done."

"I never got to say I was sorry."

"Are you?" Sarah took a sip from her cup and made a face.

Justin scowled. "What kind of question is that?"

"Well, you don't even seem to know what you did, or if you did anything."

He looked down at the laces of his sneakers, the dirty knots that he hated untangling so much that he'd just pulled the things off and on. Now they were hopeless. The knots would never come out. He sighed.

"Do you even like books?" Sarah asked. She waved her hand around. "Was all of this for her?"

"Of course I like books!" Justin said, looking up. He didn't know how to explain. He'd started library school to get Linda to Sandlin, but he actually liked it. It felt good to carefully organize the books so that other people would know what they were getting themselves into. "I've always liked books. I just don't *trust* them."

"What about people?" Sarah asked.

He looked at her blankly.

"Do you trust people?"

"I guess. I mean, sure. Within reason. I don't think people usually have terrible secrets the way characters do, but people often aren't as amazing, either. We're watered down."

"I have a secret," Sarah said. "I compete in rock, paper, scissors tournaments."

He laughed.

"I'm serious," Sarah said.

"Wait a minute. You mean you cheated me out of all that coffee?" For a moment, Justin just looked at her. She seemed different now that he knew she had secrets, even if they were kind of lame ones.

"Hey," she said. "I won fairly!"

"But you're like a pool shark or something. You have strategies."

Sarah shook her head. "Okay, you want my RPS secret? It's about understanding people. Rock's basically a weapon. Like something an ogre might hurl. It's an angry throw. Some people shy away from it because it seems crude, but they'll use it if they're desperate."

"Okay," Justin said.

"Now, scissors. Scissors are shiny and sharp. Still dangerous, but more elegant, like a rapier. Lots of people make their first throw scissors because it seems like the clever throw. The rakish throw. The hipster throw."

"Really?" Justin frowned.

"*You* threw it the first time. And the second."

He thought back, but he couldn't recall. He wondered which play Sarah usually opened up with. Was it always rock?

"Now, paper. Paper's interesting. Some people consider it a wimpy throw and they use it very infrequently. Others consider it the most subtle throw. Words can, they say, be more dangerous than rocks or scissors.

"Of course, scissors still cut paper," Sarah said.

"Oh," said Justin suddenly, getting up. "They do. You're right." He could cut Linda out like a paper doll.

700 – The Arts

Justin pulled book after book from the shelves, not caring about their spines, not caring about the mess he made, scanning each one for a mention of Linda. They piled up around him and the dust coated his hands, ink smearing his fingers as he ran them down countless pages.

Heavy metal scissors weighed down the pocket of his coat

and sometimes his hand would drop inside to touch their cool surface before emptying another shelf.

"What are you doing?" Sandlin asked.

Justin jumped up, hand still in his pocket.

Sandlin was dressed in another waistcoat. A single silver pin held a cravat in place at his neck. He sneezed.

"I'm looking for my girlfriend. She got out of her book, but I don't know which book she got into."

"The girl with all the piercings I saw you hiding with last night?"

"No," said Justin, trying not seem as rattled as he felt. *If Sandlin knew*... No, he couldn't dwell on that. "That's Sarah. Linda's my girlfriend, or she was, and she knew how to put things into books. She put herself in a Russian novel, but last night you took her out and I don't know what book she's in now."

Sandlin ran his hand over his short beard.

"You see," Justin said, his voice rising. "She could be anywhere, in danger. Novels are always putting characters in peril because it's exciting. Characters die."

"Your problem isn't with books, it's with girls," Sandlin said.

"What?" Justin demanded.

"Girls," said Sandlin. "You don't know why they do the things they do. Who does? I'm sure they feel the same about us. Hell, I'm sure they feel the same way about each other."

"But the books," said Justin.

"Fiction. I used to own a bookstore before I inherited a lot of money from my great aunt. The money went to a cat first, but when the cat died, I was loaded. Decided I'd shut my store down, sleep all day and do whatever I wanted. This is it."

"But... but what about what you said about books being alive? Needing our protection?"

Sandlin waved his hand vaguely. "Look, I love spending time with characters from books. I love the strange friendships that spring up, the romances. I don't want to lose any of them. Did you know that Naruto has become close to Edmond Dantès and a floating skull with glowing red eyes? I couldn't make that up if I tried! But it's still *fiction*. Even if it's happening in my basement. It's not real."

Justin looked at him in disbelief. "But books *feel* real. Surely they must seem more real to you than anyone. They can hurt you. They can break your heart."

"It wasn't a book," said Sandlin, "that broke your heart."

800 – Literature & Rhetoric

Justin went home and slept for the rest of the day and night. When he woke up too early to do much else, he opened a familiar paperback and re-read it. Then he went to a café and bought two cups of coffee to bring to class.

"Oh wow," said Sarah. "Double latte with a sprinkle of cinammon. I think I just drooled on myself."

"You still have to win it," he said. "You made up the rules. Now be made miserable by them."

She made a fist. "You sure you don't want to pick some game you're good at?"

Her earrings swung and glittered. Justin wondered if she wore them to tournaments to distract her opponents. He wondered if it worked.

He wished he could raise an eyebrow, but he tried to give her the look that might accompany one.

"Your funeral," said Sarah.

Rock. Paper. Scissors. Scissors cut paper. Justin won. He gave her the coffee anyway.

"I didn't think you'd throw scissors again," she said. "Since I pointed out that you threw it the first two times."

"Exactly." *See,* he thought, *I don't have a problem figuring out girls.*

Just one girl.

And possibly himself.

900 – *Geography & History*

Later that week, Justin attended the midnight party at Sandlin's house. He walked through the front door, disturbing as much dust as he could, before heading down the stairs. He arrived fashionably late. Characters were making toasts.

"*Salut!*" a group shouted together.

"To absent friends, lost loves, old gods, and the—" started another before Justin walked out of earshot.

He touched the heavy scissors in his pocket. His plan had changed.

Linda sat on a stool in black robes embroidered with the Hogwarts emblem and talked earnestly to a frog in a crown. Imps, nearby, appeared to be sticking a lit match between the stitches on the sole of a boot belonging to a chain-smoking blond man with a thick British accent.

"Linda," said Justin, "I have to talk to you."

Linda turned and something like panic crossed her face. She stood. "Justin?"

"Don't bother thanking me for bringing you to Sandlin," he said. "I won't bother saying I'm sorry. You were right. I'm glad I moved, glad I started library school. But what you did—"

"I'd always wanted to," she said. "Put myself in a book. It wasn't you. It would have happened eventually."

"Look, what I came to say was that you have responsibilities in the real world. Your parents haven't heard from you in forever. What you're doing isn't safe. You have to come back."

"No," she said firmly. "I'm not ready yet. Not now, when I can visit any book I want. I'll come out when I'm ready."

"You should have stayed and fought with me," said Justin. "It wasn't fair."

"I could have put *you* in a book." She tilted her head. "I still could."

He took an involuntary step back and she laughed.

"You don't deserve it, though," she said. "You don't love books the way that I do."

He opened his mouth to protest and then closed it. It was true. He didn't know how she loved books, only that he loved them differently.

She turned away from him and he let her go. He stayed for the rest of the party and after all the characters were back in their books, he took *Harry Potter* off the shelf.

"Found the girl?" Sandlin asked.

Justin nodded and took the scissors out of his pocket.

"What are you going to do?" Sandlin sounded nervous.

Justin turned on the old computer. "I'm going to change the story. Just a little. No one will notice." He flipped to a page where Linda's name appeared and carefully cut her out. Sandlin winced.

"Don't worry," Justin said. "It's just fiction."

He typed a few words and printed out the page. Then he carefully taped Linda's name in place so that the sentence read:

"Linda doesn't just know how to put things in books. She knows how to get things out again, including herself. Hopefully someday she will."

Folding the paper in half, he tucked it between the pages. When he left, he didn't take the book with him.

GOING IRONSIDE

LA LALA LA. THAT'S part of the song. I don't remember it all right now, but it's okay. Cally remembers the rest. So we can go back to the hill soonsoonsoon. La la. When our bellies are big as moons. Then Bucan Jack will play his fiddle and there'll be nettle wine and the Queen will ask me to tell this story a hundred hundred times.

But right now, the wall is cold against my back and I can feel the bricks shredding the gold lamé off my skirt. La lala la. The rain is cold too. Making my mascara run. I jam my hands in the pockets of my jacket, feeling the grit and the nasty tissues at the bottom.

I do a little dance, but nobody sees.

When we first came Ironside, we tried to make money out of leaves, but we didn't know what money looked like and we did it wrong. The lady at the counter started yelling, "This is Monopoly money!" Her getting red in the face just made us laugh. We thought we were so smart. We stole everything right under people's noses. Plastic skirts and dolls and lipsticks. Piles of magazines and apples with a bitter, chemical taste.

Food was the hardest. The milk tasted like iron and even the bread was bad. But now we eat caramel corn and licorice and Jolly Ranchers until we're sick.

Cally should be back soon and I'm glad, 'cause my muscles are starting to cramp all over and I already scraped the half a bag I had tucked in my shoe.

We thought we were so smart. We thought it would be easy. Just go Ironside and come back with babies. Not steal 'em either. Our babies. Elf babies. Find a boy. Roll around in the grass. Dash back. What a prank! We're no selkies. No one can grab *our* skins and keep us.

It might still work. Cally says we should give it three more months. Three's a lucky number, so I said okay. Anyway, I can't go alone. She's got the second part of the song.

I'm rubbing my arms now. They hurt. Rubbing the insides of my elbows, rubbing the bruises, singing to my veins. Soon. Soonsoonsoon.

It's easy to find boys Ironside. A touch of glamour covers your ears and eyes and all the other parts of you that might give you away. They buy you pizza and take you to parties and clubs, bring you watery drinks and drugs, and screw you in locking bathroom stalls. It was hard at first, but that's what we wanted, right? I want my elf baby, don't I?

I have a joint in my purse. I know it won't help the aches, but I light it anyway. I drag deep, fill myself up with thick smoke. Wait for Cally, I tell myself. When we go back to the hill, I'm going to bring my lighter with me. The pretty pink hologram one. Won't Bucan Jack laugh to see it! He'll love it so much that he'll make up a song just for me.

When I first got here, it was hard to breathe. All the chemicals and the iron, you can feel it, smell it. Molten and roiling. It sticks to your skin and makes you so heavy that you have to lie down. Magic's hard, Ironside, even trifling stuff, and the longer you're here, the more you forget. Even the leaf trick doesn't work anymore. But other things are a lot better. Like when I take a breath, all I smell is the marijuana smoke, the tar of the asphalt, spoiled food, and me, reeking of vomit. I need a bath soon.

Everything is soon, but nothing is nownownow.

I want a baby with crow black eyes and lips like plums. I want Cally to come back with my five bags of brown stuff—good stuff—so I can stop shivering and cramping out here in the rain. I want to go dancing, not at a club, but out there—in a lawn or park, someplace green, just me and Cally.

And Cally, if you come back now, I promise I'll make the bags last this time. I will. I'll space it out. Just enough to stop the aches. Just enough for three more months. We'll do it your way. I'm willing. More than willing. Just bring me back my dope.

The insides of my arms are little pursed mouths and the needle in my bag is a snake, rolling and flapping against the sides of my handbag, rattling, making me want to shoot up water just to fake my arms out. And the single fang is iron, making black burns where it touches, but it is a good burn. I need that burn.

Do you remember the time we put knots in the horses' manes before the last rade? Or how about the madcap chase when we stole that grindylow's cap? It was you, me, and Jack that time. Do you remember? Lala la la la la.

I do another little dance, but this one is more like a shuffle. I don't care if nobody sees. I don't care.

You aren't back yet, Cally, but I won't worry. You could easily be stretched out, languid and sated, in the back of a car. Thick-necked Tom beside you, his gold-ringed fingers picking your pockets while that shrew-guy, I forget his name, drives. I hope not, Cally. Be careful. I need it. Put it in the one thing they won't want you to open. Put it in your mouth.

I watch the rain-soaked headlights come towards me and fly past. Which one is you? I do a little turn on my toe and slip but don't fall. Not yet. I wonder if anyone will stop and ask me if I need a date? A fix? A ride?

Oh Cally, I'm thinking about Jack again, him standing on his head or teasing you. Does he wonder where we got to? Does he miss us? Oh, sure, he heard us talk, but did he think we'd really do it? Did he think we were smart, crazy smart, sharp as nails, as tacks, as the needle in my bag?

Didja? Didja think it, Jack? Did you think we could do it, go between, go Ironside and get ourselves elf babies? But then maybe you don't miss us at all, do you? Time's different here. You don't even know we're gone. A hundred hundred years will pass for you in one sleepy day without me.

The Land of Heart's Desire

If you want to meet real-life members of the Sidhe—real faeries—go to the café, Moon in a Cup, in Manhattan. Faeries congregate there in large numbers. You can tell them by the slight point of their ears—a feature they're too arrogant to conceal by glamour—and by their inhuman grace. You will also find that the café caters to their odd palate by offering nettle and foxglove teas, ragwort pastries. Please note too that foxglove is poisonous to mortals and shouldn't be tasted by you.

— posted in messageboard www.realfairies.com/forums by stoneneil

LORDS OF FAERIE SOMETIMES walk among us. Even in places stinking of cold iron, up broken concrete steps, in tiny apartments where girls sleep three to a bedroom. Faeries, after all, delight in corruption, in borders, in crossing over and then crossing back again.

When Rath Roiben Rye, Lord of the Unseelie Court and Several Other Places, comes to see Kaye, she drags her mattress into the middle of the living room so that they can talk until dawn without waking anyone. Kaye isn't human either, but she was raised human. Sometimes, to Roiben, she seems more human than the city around her.

In the mornings, her roommates Ruth and Val (if she's not staying with her boyfriend) and Corny (who sleeps in their walk-in closet, although he calls it "the second bedroom") step over them. Val grinds coffee and brews it in a French press with lots of cinnamon. She shaved her head a year ago and her rust-colored hair is finally long enough that it's starting to curl.

Kaye laughs and drinks out of chipped mugs and lets her long green pixie fingers trace patterns on Roiben's skin. In those moments, with the smell of her in his throat, stronger than all the iron of the world, he feels as raw and trembling as something newly born.

One day in midsummer, Roiben took on a mortal guise and went to Moon in a Cup in the hope that Kaye's shift might soon be over. He thought they would walk through Riverside Park and look at the reflection of lights on the water. Or eat nuts rimed with salt. Or whatsoever else she wanted. He needed those memories of her to sustain him when he returned to his own kingdoms.

But walking in just after sunset, black coat flapping around his ankles like crow wings, he could see she wasn't there. The coffeeshop was full of mortals, more full than usual. Behind the counter, Corny ran back and forth, banging mugs in a cloud of espresso steam.

The coffee shop had been furnished with things Kaye and her human friends had found by the side of the road or at cheap tag sales. Lots of ratty paint-stained little wooden tables that she'd decoupaged with post cards, sheets of music, and pages from old encyclopedias. Lots of chairs painted gold. The walls were hung with amateur paintings, framed in scrap metal. Even the cups were mismatched. Delicate bone china cups sitting on saucers beside mugs with slogans for businesses long closed.

As Roiben walked to the back of the shop, several of the patrons gave him appraising glances. In the reflection of the shining copper coffee urn, he looked as he always did. His white hair was pulled back. His eyes were the color of the silver spoons. He wondered if he should alter his guise.

"Where is she?" Roiben asked.

"Imperious, aren't we?" Corny shouted over the roar of the machine. "Well, whatever magical booty call the king of the faeries is after will have to wait. I have no idea where Kaye's at. All I know is that she should be here."

Roiben tried to control the sharp flush of annoyance that made his hand twitch for a blade.

"I'm sorry," Corny said, rubbing his hand over his face. "That was uncool. Val said she'd come help but she's *not* here and Luis, who's *supposed* to be my boyfriend, is off with some study partner for hours and hours and my scheme to get some more business has backfired in a big way. And then you come in here and you're so—you're always so—"

"May I get myself some nettle tea to bide with?" Roiben

interrupted, frowning. "I know where you keep it. I will attend to myself."

"You can't," Corny said, waving him around the back of the bar. "I mean, you could have, but they drank it all, and I don't know how to make more."

Behind the bar was a mess. Roiben bent to pick up the cracked remains of a cup and frowned. "What's going on here? Since when have mortals formed a taste for—"

"Excuse me," said a girl with long wine-colored hair. "Are you human?"

He froze, suddenly conscious of the jagged edges of what he held. "I'm supposing I misheard you." He set the porcelain fragment down discreetly on the counter.

"You're one of them, aren't you? I knew it!" A huge smile split her face and she looked back eagerly toward a table of grinning humans. "Can you grant wishes?"

Roiben looked at Corny, busy frothing milk. "Cornelius," he said softly. "Um."

Corny glanced over. "If, for once, you just act like my best friend's boyfriend and take her order, I promise to be nicer to you. Nice to you, even."

Roiben touched a key on the register. "I'll do it if you promise to be more afraid of me."

"I envy what I fear and hate what I envy," Corny said, slamming an iced latte on the counter. "More afraid equals more of a jerk."

"What is it you'd like?" Roiben asked the girl. "Other than wishes."

"Soy mocha," said the girl. "But please, there's so much I want to know."

Roiben squinted at the scrawled menu on the chalkboard. "Payment, if you please."

She counted out some bills and he took them, looking helplessly at the register. He hit a few buttons and, to his relief, the drawer opened. He gave her careful change.

"Please tell me that you didn't pay her in leaves and acorns," Corny said. "Kaye keeps doing that and it's really not helping business."

"I knew it!" said the girl.

"I conjured nothing," Roiben said. "And you are not helping."

Corny squirted out Hershey's syrup into the bottom of a mug. "Yeah, remember what I said about my idea to get Moon in a Cup more business?"

Roiben crossed his arms over his chest. "I do."

"I might have posted online that this place has a high incidence of supernatural visitation."

Roiben narrowed his eyes and tilted his head. "You claimed Kaye's coffee shop is haunted?"

The girl picked up her mocha from the counter. "He said that faeries came here. Real faeries. The kind that dance in mushroom circles and—"

"Oh, did he?" Roiben asked, a snarl in his voice. "That's what he said?"

Corny didn't want to be jealous of the rest of them.

He didn't want to spend his time wondering how long it would be before Luis got tired of him. Luis, who was going places while Corny helped Kaye open Moon in a Cup because he had literally nothing else to do.

Kaye ran the place like a pixie. It had odd hours—sometimes opening at four in the afternoon, sometimes opening at dawn. The service was equally strange when Kaye was behind the counter. A cappuccino would be ordered and chai tea would be delivered. People's change often turned to leaves and ash. Slowly—for survival—things evolved so that Moon in a Cup belonged to all of them. Val and Ruth worked when they weren't at school. Corny set up the wireless.

And Luis, who lived in the dorms of NYU and was busy with a double major and flirting with a future in medicine, would come and type out his long papers at one of the tables to make the place look more full.

But it wouldn't survive like that for long, Corny knew. Everything was too precarious. Everyone else had too much going on. So he made the decision to run the ad. And for a week straight, the coffee shop had been full of people. They could barely make the drinks in time. So none of the others could be mad at him. They had no right to be mad at him.

He had to stay busy. It was the only way to keep the horrible gnawing dread at bay.

Roiben listened to Corny stammer through an explanation of what he had done and why without really hearing it.

Then he made himself tea and sat at one of the salvaged tables that decorated the coffeehouse. Its surface was ringed with marks from the tens of dozens of watery cups that had rested there and any weight made the whole thing rock alarmingly. He took a sip of the foxglove tea—brewed by his own hand to be strong and bitter.

Val had come in during Corny's explanation, blanched, and started sweeping the floor. Now she and Corny whispered together behind the counter, Val shaking her head.

Faeries had, for many years, relied on discretion. Roiben knew the only thing keeping Corny from torment at the hands of the faeries who must have seen his markedly indiscreet advertisement was the implied protection of the King of the Unseelie Court. Roiben knew it and resented it.

It would be an easy thing to withdraw his protection. Easy and perhaps just.

As he considered that, a woman's voice behind him rose, infuriating him further. "Well, you see, my family has always been close to the faeries. My great great great great grandmother was even stolen away to live with them."

Roiben wondered why mortals so wanted to be associated with suffering that they told foolish tales. Why not tell a story where one's grandmother died fat, old and beloved by her dozen children?

"Really?" the woman's friend was saying. "Like Robert Kirk on the faerie hill?"

"Exactly," said the woman. "Except that Great Grandma Clarabelle wasn't sleeping outdoors and she was right here in New York State. She got taken out of her own bed! Clarabelle had just given birth to a stillborn baby and the priest came too late to baptize her. No iron over the doors."

It happened like that sometimes, he had to concede.

"*Oh*," her friend said, shaking her head. "Yes, we've forgotten about iron and salt and all the other protections."

Clara. For a moment, thoughts of Corny and his betrayal went out of Roiben's head completely. He knew that name. And although there have been dozens upon dozens of Claras who have come into the world, in that moment, he knew the women were telling a true story. A story he knew. It shamed him that he had dismissed them so easily for being foolish. Even fools tell the truth. Historically, the truth belongs especially to fools.

"Excuse me," Roiben said, turning in his chair. "I couldn't help overhearing."

"Do you believe in faeries?" she asked him, seeming pleased.

"I'm afraid I must," he said, finally. "May I ask you something about Clara?"

"My great great aunt," the woman said, smiling. "I'm named after her. I'm Clarabella. Well, it's really my middle name, but I still—"

"A pleasure to make your acquaintance," he said, extending his hand to shake hers. "Do you happen to know when your Clara went missing?"

"Some time in the eighteenth century, I guess," she said. Her voice slowed as she got to the end of the sentence, as though she'd become wary. Her smile dimmed. "Is something the matter?"

"And did she have two children?" he asked recklessly. "A boy named Robert and a girl named Mary?"

"How could you have known that?" Clarabella said, her voice rising.

"I didn't know it," Roiben said. "That is the reason I asked."

"But you—you shouldn't have been able to—"

Everyone in the coffeeshop was staring at them now. Roiben perceived a goblin by the door, snickering as he licked chocolate icing from his fingers.

Her friend put a hand on Clarabella's arm. "He's one of the fair folk," she said, hushed. "Be careful. He might want to steal you, too."

Roiben laughed, suddenly, but his throat felt full of thorns.

It is eternal summer in the Seelie Court, as changeless as faeries themselves. Trees hang eternally heavy with golden fruit and flowering vines climb walls to flood bark-shingled roofs with an endless rain of petals.

Roiben recalled being a child there, growing up in indolent pleasure and carelessness. He and his sister Ethine lived far from the faeries who'd sired them and thought no more of them than they thought of the sunless sky or of the patterns that the pale fishes in the stream made with their mad darting.

They had games to amuse themselves with. They dissected grasshoppers, they pulled the wings from moths and sewed them to the backs of toads to see if they could make the toads fly. And when they tired of those games they had a nurse called Clara with which to play.

She had mud brown hair and eyes as green as wet pools. In her more lucid moments, she hated her faerie charges. She must have known that she had been stolen away from home, from her own family and children, to care for beings she considered little better than soulless devils. When Ethine and Roiben would clamour for her lap, she thrust them away. When they teased her for her evening prayers, she described how their skin would crackle and smoke, as they roasted in hell after the final judgment day.

She could be kind, too. She taught them songs and chased them through meadows until they shrieked with laughter. They played fox and geese with acorns and holes dug by their fingers in the dirt. They played charades and forfeits. They played graces with hoops and sticks woven from willow trees. And after, Clara washed their dirty cheeks with her handkerchief, dipped in the water of the stream, and made up beds for them in the moss.

And when she kissed their clean faces and bid them goodnight, she would call them Robert and Mary. Her lost children. The children that she had been enchanted to think they were.

Roiben did not remember pitying Clara then, although thinking back on it, he found her pitiable. He and Ethine were young and their love for her was too selfish to want anything more than to be loved best. They hated being called by another's name and pinched her in punishment or hid from her until she wept.

One day, Ethine said that she'd come up with a plan to make Clara forget all about Robert and Mary. Roiben gathered up the mushrooms, just as his sister told him.

He didn't know that what was wholesome to him might poison Clara.

They killed her, by accident, as easily as they had pulled the wings from the moth or stabbed the grasshopper. Eventually, their faerie mother came and laughed at their foolishness and staged a beautiful funeral. Ethine had woven garlands to hang around the neck of Clara's corpse and no one washed their cheeks, even when they got smeared with mud.

And although the funeral was amusing and their faerie mother an entertaining novelty, Roiben could not stop thinking of the way Clara had looked at him as she died. As if, perhaps, she had loved her monstrous faerie children after all, and in that moment, regretted it. It was a familiar look, one that he had long thought was love but now recognized as hatred.

Corny watched Val foam milk and wondered if he should go home. The crowd was starting to die down and they could probably close in an hour or two. He was almost exhausted enough to be able to crawl into bed and let his body's need for sleep overtake his mind's need to race around in helpless circles.

Then Corny looked up and saw Roiben on his feet, staring at some poor woman like he was going to rip off her head. Corny had no idea what the lady had said, but if the girl at the counter was any indication, it could have been pretty crazy. He left a customer trying to decide whether or not she really wanted an extra shot of elderflower syrup to rush across the coffee shop.

"Everything okay over here?" Corny asked. Roiben flinched, like he hadn't noticed Corny getting so close and had to restrain some violent impulse.

"This woman was telling a story about her ancestor," Roiben said tightly, voice full of false pleasure. "A story that perhaps she read somewhere or which has been passed down through her family. About how a woman named Clarabelle was taken away by the faeries. I simply want to hear the whole thing."

Corny turned to the woman. "Okay, you two. Get out of here. Now." He pushed her and her friend toward the door.

They went, pulling on their coats and looking back nervously, like they wanted to complain but didn't dare.

"As for you," Corny said to Roiben, trying to keep from seeming as nervous as he now felt. His hands were sweating. "People are idiots. So she made up some ridiculous story? It doesn't matter. You don't need to do . . . whatever it is you're thinking of doing to her."

"No," Roiben said and Corny cringed automatically.

"Please just let—" Corny started, but Roiben cut him off.

His voice was steely and his eyes looked like chips of ice. "Mortal, you are trying my patience. This is all *your* doing. Were I to merely turn my back, they would come for you, they would drag you through the skies and torment you until madness finally, mercifully robbed you of your senses."

"You're a real charmer," Corny said, but his voice shook.

The door opened, bell ringing, and they both half-turned toward it. *He's looking for Kaye,* Corny thought. If she came through the door, she could charm Roiben into forgetting to be angry.

But it wasn't Kaye. Luis walked through the door with three college guys, backpacks and messenger bags slung over their shoulders. Luis took a quick look in Corny's direction, then walked to the table with them, dumped his bag.

"Come with me," Roiben said quietly.

"Where are we going?" Corny asked.

"There are always consequences. It's time for you to face yours."

Corny nodded, helpless to do anything else. He took a deep breath and let himself be guided to the door.

"Leave him alone," Luis said. Corny turned to find that Luis was holding Roiben's wrist. The welts in Luis's brown skin where the Night Court had ripped out his iron piercings, loop by loop, had healed to scars, but Luis's single cloudy eye, put out by a faerie because Luis had the Sight, would never get better.

Roiben raised one pale brow. He looked more amused than worried. Maybe he was angry enough to hope for an excuse to hurt someone.

"Don't worry about me," Corny told Luis stiffly. "I'll be right back. Go back to your friends."

Luis frowned and Corny silently willed him to go away. There was no point in both of them getting in trouble.

"You're not getting him without a fight," Luis said quietly.

"I mislike your tone," said Roiben, pulling his wrist free with a sudden twist of his arm. "Cornelius and I have some things to discuss. It's naught to do with you."

Luis turned to Corny. "You told him about the ad? Are you an idiot?"

"He figured it out for himself," Corny said.

"Is that all, Luis? Have we your permission to go outside?" Roiben asked.

"I'm going with you," Luis said.

"No you're not." Corny shoved at Luis' shoulder, harder than he'd intended. "You're never around for anything else, why be around for this? Go back to your friends. Why don't you go study with them or whatever you do? Go back and admit you're sick of me already. I bet you never even told them you had a boyfriend."

Luis blanched.

"That's what I thought," Corny said. "Just break up with me already."

"What's wrong with you?" asked Luis. "Are you really going to be pissed off at people who you've never met—just because I go to school with them? You hate them, that's why I don't tell them about you."

"I hate them because they're what you want me to be," Corny said. "Nagging me to register for classes. Wanting me to stay clear of faeries even though my best friend is one. Wanting me to be someone I'm never going to be."

Luis looked shocked, like each word was a slap. "All I want is for you not to get yourself killed."

"I don't need your pity," Corny said and pushed through the door, leaving Roiben to follow him. It felt good, the adrenaline rushing through his veins. It felt like setting the whole world on fire.

"Wait," Luis called from behind him. "Don't go."

But it was too late to turn back. Corny walked out of the warm coffee shop, onto the sidewalk and then turned into the mouth of the dark, stinking alley that ran next to Moon in a Cup. He heard Roiben's relentless footsteps approaching.

Corny leaned his forehead against the cold brick wall and closed his eyes. "I really screwed that up, didn't I?"

"You said that you envied what you feared and hated what you envied." Roiben rested his long fingers on Corny's shoulder. "But it is as easy to hate what you love as to hate what you fear."

Roiben leaned against the wall of the alley, unsure of what else to say. His own rage at himself and his memories had dulled in the face of Corny's obvious misery. He had already come up with a vague idea for a fitting punishment, but it seemed cruel to do it now. Of course, perhaps cruelty should be the point.

"I don't know what's wrong with me," Corny said, head bent so that Roiben could see the nape of his neck, already covered in gooseflesh. Corny had left Moon in a Cup without his jacket and his thin T-shirt was no protection against the wind.

"You were only trying to keep him safe," Roiben said. "I think even he knows it."

Corny shook his head. "No, I wanted to hurt him. I wanted to hurt him before he got a chance to hurt me. I'm ruining our relationship and I just don't know how to stop myself."

"I'm hardly the person to advise you," Roiben said stiffly. "Recall Silarial. I have more than once mistaken hate for love. I have no wisdom here."

"Oh, come on," Corny said. "You're my best friend's boyfriend. You must talk to her sometimes—you must talk to her like this."

"Not like this," Roiben said, not without irony. But in truth the way that Corny was speaking felt dangerous, as though one's feelings might only continue to work if they remained undisturbed.

"Look, you seem grim and miserable most of the time, but I know you love her."

"Of course I love her," Roiben snapped.

"How can you?" Corny asked. He took a deep breath and spoke again, so quickly that the words tumbled over one another.

"How can you *trust* someone that much? I mean, she's just going to hurt you, right? What if someday she just stops liking you? What if she finds someone else—" Corny stopped abruptly, and Roiben realized he was frowning ominously. His fingers had dug into the pads of his own palms.

"Go on," Roiben said, deliberately relaxing his body.

Corny ran a hand through his dyed black hair. "She's going to eventually get tired of putting up with you never being around when the important stuff is going on, never changing while she's figuring out her own life. Eventually, you'll just be a shadow."

Roiben found that he'd been clenching his jaw so tightly that his teeth ached. It was everything he was afraid of, laid before him like a feast of ashes.

"That's what I feel like I'm like. Going nowhere while Luis has gone from living on the street to some fancy university. He's going to be a doctor someday—a real one—and what am I going to be?"

Roiben nodded slowly. He'd forgotten they were talking about Corny and Luis.

"So how do you do it?" Corny demanded. "How do you love someone when you don't know if it's forever or not? When he might just leave you?"

"Kaye is the only thing that saves me from myself," Roiben said.

Corny turned at that and narrowed his eyes. "What do you mean?"

Roiben shook his head, unsure of how to express any of his tangled thoughts. "I hadn't recalled her in a long time—Clara. When I was a child, I had a human nurse enchanted to serve me.

She couldn't love me." Roiben hesitated. "She couldn't love me, because she had no choices. She wasn't free to love me. She never had a chance. I too have been enchanted to serve. I understand her better now."

He felt a familiar revulsion thinking of his past, thinking of captivity with Nicnevin, but he pushed past it to speak. "After all the humiliations I have suffered, all the things I have done for my mistresses at their commands, here I am in a dirty human restaurant, serving coffee to fools. For Kaye. Because I am free to. Because I think it would please her. Because I think it would make her laugh."

"It's definitely going to make her laugh," Corny said.

"Thus I am saved from my own grim self," Roiben said, shrugging his shoulders, a small smile lifting his mouth.

Corny laughed. "So you're saying the world is cold and bleak, but infinitesimally less bleak with Kaye around? Could you *be* any more depressing?"

Roiben tilted his head. "And yet, here you are, more miserable than I."

"Funny." Corny made a face.

"Look, you can make someone appear to love you," Roiben said as carefully as he had put the jagged piece of broken china on the counter. "By enchantment or more subtle cruelties. You could cripple him such that he would forget that he had other choices."

"That's not what I want," Corny said.

Roiben smiled. "Are you sure?"

"Are *you*? Yes, I'm sure," Corny said hotly. "I just don't want to keep anticipating the worst. If it's going to be over tomorrow, then let it be over right now so I can get on with the pain and disappointment."

"If there is nothing but this," Roiben said. "If we are to be shadows, changeless and forgotten, we will have to dine on these memories for the rest of our days. Don't you want a few more moments to chew over?"

Corny shivered. "That's horrible. You're supposed to say that I'm wrong."

"I'm only repeating your words." Roiben brushed silver hair back from his face.

"But you believe them," said Corny. "You actually think that's what's going to happen with you and Kaye."

Roiben smiled gently. "And you're not the fatalist you pretend. What was it you said? *More afraid equals more of a jerk.* You're afraid, nothing more."

Corny snorted a little when Roiben said *jerk.*

"Yeah, I guess," he said, looking down at the asphalt and the strewn garbage. "But I can't *stop* being afraid."

"Perhaps, then, you could address the jerk part," Roiben said. "Or perhaps you could tell Luis, so he could at least try to reassure you."

Corny tilted his head, as if he was seeing Roiben for the first time. "You're afraid, too."

"Am I?" Roiben asked, but there was something in Cornelius's face that he found unnerving. He wondered what Corny thought he was looking at.

"I bet you're afraid you'll start hoping, despite your best intentions," Corny said. "You're okay with doom and gloom, but I bet it's really scary to think things might work out. I bet it's fucking terrifying to think she might love you the way you love her."

"Mayhaps." Roiben tried not to let anything show on his face. "Either way, before we go back inside I have a geas to place on you. Something to remind you of why you ought keep secrets secret."

"Oh come on," said Corny with a groan. "What about our meaningful talk? Aren't we friends now? Don't we get to do each other's nails and overlook each other's small, amusing betrayals?"

Roiben reached out one cold hand. "Afraid not."

Kaye was sitting on the counter of Moon in a Cup, looking annoyed, when Corny and Roiben walked back through the doors. Catching sight of them, her expression went slack with astonishment.

Luis, beside her, choked on a mouthful of hot chocolate and needed to be slapped several times on the back by Val before he recovered himself.

Cornelius's punishment was simple. Roiben had glamoured him to have small bone-pale horns jutting from his temples and had given his skin a light blue sheen. His ears tapered to delicate points. The glamour would last a single month—from one fat, full moon to the next. And when he made coffee, he would have to face all those hopeful faerie seekers.

"I guess I deserve this," Corny said to no one in particular.

"Why did I even try to save you?" Luis said. Though his friends had gone, he was still there, still patiently waiting. Roiben hoped that Corny noticed that before all else.

Kaye walked toward Roiben. "I bet I know what you've been thinking," she said, shaking her head. "Bad things."

"Never when you're here," he told her, but he wasn't sure she heard as her arm wrapped around his waist so she could smother her helpless giggling against his chest. He drank in the warmth of her and tried, for once, to believe this could all last.

The Poison Eaters

I TRUST THAT YOUR bonds are not too tight, my son. Please don't struggle. Don't bother. You're soft. All princes are soft, and these cells are built for hardened men.

It is a shame that you never met your grandmother. You are very like with your tempers and your rages. I imagine she would have doted on you. How ironic that Father tried her for being a poisoner. Right now, especially, Paul, I imagine irony is much on your mind.

The morning of her execution she had her attendants dress her all in red and braid her hair with fresh roses. Wine-colored stones cluttered her fingers. There are several paintings of it; she died opulently. It was drizzling. I was to walk her to her tomb. It was something like a wedding processional as she took my arm and we went together, down the steep steps. The place was dark and stank of incense. My mother leaned close to me and whispered that I looked splendid in black. I remember not being able to say anything, only taking her hand and pressing it. Outside, the rain began to fall hard. We heard the shrieks of the assemblage; aristocrats don't like to be wet.

My mother smiled and said, "I bet they wish they were down here where it's dry."

I forced a smile and made myself kiss her cheek and bid her farewell. The masons were waiting at the top of the stairs.

My mother and I were not close, but she was still my mother. I was a dutiful son. I had commanded the cooks to put the sharpest of my hunting knives beneath the food they had prepared for her. I wonder if you would do that for me, Paul. Perhaps you would. After all, it cost me nothing to be kind.

See this cup? A beautiful thing, solid gold, one of the few treasures of our family that remains. It was my father's. He had a cupbearer bring him his wine in it, even as his other guests drank from silver. I have it here beside me, just as you filled it—half with poison and half with cider, so that it will go down easy.

I have a story to tell you. You've always been restless, too busy to hear stories of people long dead and secrets that no longer matter. But now, Paul, bound and gagged as you are, you can hardly object to my telling you a tale:

Sometimes at night the three sisters would sleep in one bed, limbs tangling together. Despite that, they would never get warm. Their lips would stay blue and sometimes one of them would shake or cramp, but they were used to that. Sometimes, in the mornings, when women would bring them their breakfasts, one might touch them by accident and the next day she would be missing. But they were used to that, too. Not that they did not grieve. They often wept. They wept over the mice they would find, stiff and cold, on the stone floor of their chamber; over the hunting dogs that would run to them when they were out walking on the hills, jumping up and then falling down; over the butterfly that once landed on Mirabelle's cheek for a moment, before spiraling to the ground like a bit of paper.

One winter, their father gave them lockets. Each locket had the painting of a boy inside of it. They took turns making up stories about the boys. In one story, Alice's picture, who they'd taken to calling Nicholas, was a knight with a silver arm, questing after a sword cooled from its forge with the blood of sirens. At night, the sword became a siren with hair as black as ink and Nicholas fell in love with her. At this point the story stopped because Alice stormed off, annoyed that Cecily had made up a story where the boy from her locket fell in love with someone else.

Each day they would eat a salad of what looked like flowering parsley. Afterwards, their hands would tremble and they would become so cold that they had to sit close to the fire and scorch themselves. Sometimes their father came in and watched them eat, but he was careful to never touch them. Instead, he would read them prayers or lecture on the dangers of sloth and the importance of needlework. Occasionally, he would have one of them read from Homer.

Summer was their favorite time. The sun would warm their sluggish blood and they would lie out in the garden like snakes. It was on one of those jaunts that the blacksmith's apprentice first spotted Alice. He started coming around a lot after that, reading his weepy poetry and trying to get her to pay him attention. Before long, Alice was always crying. She wanted to go to him, but she dared not.

"He's not the boy in your locket," Mirabelle said.

"Don't be stupid." Alice wiped her reddened eyes. "Do you think that we're supposed to marry them and be their wives? Do you think that's why we have those lockets?"

Cecily had been about to say something and stopped. She'd always thought the boys in the lockets would be theirs someday, but she did not want to say so now, in case Alice called her stupid too.

"Imagine any of us married. What would happen then, sisters? We are merely knives in the process of being sharpened."

"Why would Father do that?" Cecily demanded.

"Father?" Alice demanded. "Do you really think he's your father? Or mine? Look at us. How could you, Mirabelle, be short and fair while Cecily is tall and dark? How could I have breasts like melons, while hers are barely currants? How could we all be so close in age? We three are no more sisters than he is our father."

Mirabelle began to weep. They went to bed that night in silence, but when they awoke, Mirabelle would no longer eat. She spit out her bitter greens, even when she became tired and languid. Cecily begged her to take something, telling her that they were sisters no matter what.

"Different mothers could explain our looks," Alice said, but she did not sound convinced and Mirabelle would not be comforted.

Their father tried to force Mirabelle to eat, but she pushed food into her cheek only to spit it out again when he was gone. She got thinner and more wan, her body shriveling, but she did not die. She faded into a thin wispy thing, as ephemeral as smoke.

"What does it mean?" Cecily asked.

"It means she shouldn't be so foolish," said their father. He tried to tempt her with a frond of bitter herb in a gloved hand, but she was so insubstantial that she passed through him without causing harm and drifted out to the gardens.

"It's my fault," said Alice.

But the ghostly shape of Mirabelle merely laughed her whispery laugh.

The next day Alice went out to meet the blacksmith's apprentice and kissed him until he died. It did not bring her sister back. It did not help her grief. She built a fire and threw herself on it. She burned until she was only a blackened shadow.

No tears were enough to express how Cecily felt, so her eyes remained dry as her sisters floated like shades through the halls of the estate and her father locked himself in his study.

As Cecily sat alone in a dim room, her sisters came to her.

"You must bury us," Alice said.

"I want it to be in the gardens of one of our suitors. Together, so that we won't be lonely."

"Why should I? Why should I do anything for you?" Cecily asked. "You left me here alone."

"Stop feeling sorry for yourself," said Alice. Lack of corporeal form had not made her any less bossy.

"We need you," Mirabelle pleaded.

"Why can't you bury yourselves? Just drift down into the dirt."

"That's not the way it works," Mirabelle told her.

And so, with a sigh of resignation, gathering up the lockets of her sisters, Cecily left the estate and began to walk. She was not sure where she was headed, but the road led to town.

It was frightening to be on her own, with no one to brush her hair or tell her when to sit down to lunch. The forest sounded strange and ominous.

She stopped and paid for an apple with a silver ring. As she passed a stall, she overheard one of the merchants say. "Look at her blue mouth, her pale skin. She's the walking dead." As soon as he said it, Cecily knew it to be true. That was why Alice and Mirabelle would not die. They were already dead.

She walked for a long time, resting by a stream when she was tired. After she rose, she saw the imprint of herself in the withered grass. Tears rolled over her cheeks and dampened the cloth of her dress, but one fell where ants scurried and stilled them. After that, Cecily was careful not to cry.

At the next town, she showed the pictures in each of the lockets to the woman who sold wreaths for graves. She knew only the first boy. His name was Vance—not Nicholas—and he was the son of a wealthy landowner to the East who had once paid her for a hundred wreaths of chrysanthemums to decorate the necks of horses on Vance's twelfth birthday.

She started down the winding and dusty road East. Once she was given a ride on a wagon filled with hay. She kept her hands folded in her lap and when the farmer reached out to touch her shoulder in kindness, she shied away as though she despised him. The coldness in his eyes afterward hurt her and she tried not to think of him.

Another traveler demanded the necklace of opals she wore at her throat, but she slapped him and he fell, as if struck by a blow more terrible than any her soft hand should have delivered.

Her sisters chattered at her as she went. Sometimes their

words buzzed around her like hornets, sometimes they went sulkily silent. Once, Mirabelle and Alice had a fight about which of their deaths was more foolish and Cecily had to shout at them until they stopped.

Cecily often got hungry, but there was no salad of bitter parsley, so she ate other leaves and flowers she picked in the woods. Some of them filled her with that familiar cold shakiness while others went down her throat without doing anything but sating her. She drank from cool streams and muddy puddles and by the time she reached Vance's estate, her shoes were riddled with holes.

The manor house was at the top of a small hill and the path was set with smooth, pale stones. The door was a deep red, the color berries stained eager fingers. Cecily rapped on the door.

The servants saw her tattered finery and brought her to Master Hornpull. He had white hair that fell to his shoulders but the top of his pate was bald, shining with oil, and slightly sunburnt.

Cecily showed him the locket with Vance's picture and told him about Alice's death. He was kind and did not mention the state of Cecily's clothing or the strangeness of her coming so suddenly and on foot. He told servants to prepare a room for her and let her wash herself in a tub with golden faucets in the shape of swans.

"If you kiss him once, then I will be able to kiss him forever and ever," Alice told her as she dried off.

"I thought you liked the blacksmith's apprentice," Cecily said.

"I always liked Nicholas better." Alice's ghostly voice sounded snappish.

"Vance," Cecily corrected.

Servants came to ask Cecily if she would go to dinner, but she begged off, pleading weariness. She planned to doze on the down mattress until nightfall when she could steal out to the gardens, but there was a sharp rap on the door and her father walked into the room.

Cecily made a poorly concealed gasp and struggled to stand. For a moment, she was afraid, without really knowing why.

He pushed back graying hair with a gloved hand. "How fortunate that you are so predictable. I was quite worried when I found you had gone."

"I was too sad to be there alone," Cecily said. She could not meet his eyes.

"'You must marry Vance in Alice's place.'

"I can't," Cecily said. What she meant was that Alice would be mad, and indeed, Alice was already darting around, muttering furiously.

"You can and you will," her father said. "Every thing yearns to do what it is made for."

Cecily said nothing. He drew from his pocket a necklace of tourmalines and fastened them at her throat. "Be as good a girl as you are lovely," he said. "Then we will go home."

The earliest memory Cecily had of her father was of gloved hands, mail-over-leather, checking her gums. She had been very sick for a long time, lying on mounds of hay in a stinking room full of sick little girls. She remembered his messy hair and his perfectly trimmed beard and the way his smile had seemed aimed in her direction but not for her. "Little girls are like oysters," he told her as he pried her eyelids wide. "Just as a grain of sand irritates the oyster into making nacre, so your discomfort will make something marvelous."

"Who are you?" she had asked him.

"Don't you remember?" he had said. "I'm your father."

That had upset her, because she must be very sick indeed to not know her own father, but he told her that she had died and come back to life, so it was natural that she'd forgotten things. He lifted her up with his gloved hands and carried her out of the room. She remembered seeing other sick girls on the hay, their eyes sunken and dull and their bodies very still. That, she wouldn't have minded forgetting.

Cecily thought of those girls as she drifted off to sleep in the vast and silky bed Master Hornpull provided for her, cooled by the twining limbs of her ghostly sisters.

The next day, Cecily's face was painted with brushes: her mouth made vermillion, her eyelids smeared with cerulean, her cheeks rouged rose. They had brought pots of white stuff to smear on her skin but she was already so pale there was no need. Cecily waved the servants off and pinned up her hair herself. She wasn't very good at it and locks tumbled down over her shoulders. Mirabelle assured her that it looked better that way. Alice told her that she looked like a mess. Mirabelle said that Alice was just jealous. That might have been true; Alice had always been a jealous person.

In the parlor downstairs, Cecily's father grabbed her elbow with one gloved hand and spoke through a broad, forced smile.

Vance was nothing like their made-up stories. He was short and slender, but handsome just the same. They danced and Cecily was conscious of the warmth of his hands though the fabric of her dress and the satin of her gloves, but she was even more conscious of the tender glances he gave to a small, curvy girl in a golden gown.

"He would have liked me," Alice crowed. "I am exactly the kind of girl he likes."

"Maybe you should have thought of that before you—" Cecily started, forgetting for a moment that she was speaking to the dead. Vance turned toward her, face flaming and lips spilling apology. He must have thought she was offended that someone else caught his eye.

But when the priest asked Cecily to take Vance in marriage, she was named as Mirabelle. She repeated the words anyway.

"Does that mean Nicholas is mine?" Mirabelle whispered, her ghostly voice filled with surprised delight. He was her clear favorite in the stories. Cecily had made the boy in Mirabelle's locket too bookish for her tastes.

"Vance," Cecily corrected under her breath.

"Kill him already," Alice hissed. "Stop mooning around."

And, indeed, Vance was leaning toward Cecily to seal their vows with a kiss. She pulled back at the last moment, so that his mouth merely brushed her veil, then tried to smile in apology. As she turned to depart the ceremony with her new husband, she saw her father in the crowd. He nodded once in her direction.

At the party following the wedding, one of the guests remarked to Cecily how good it was that her father was taking an interest in society again, after falling out of favor with the King.

"He seldom talks to me about politics," Cecily said. "I did not know he was ever a friend of his Majesty."

The woman who had said it looked around, seemingly torn

between guilt and gossip. "Well, it was when the King was only the youngest Prince. No one expected him to take the throne, because his father was so young and his two older brothers so healthy. But illness took all three of them, one after another, and once his Majesty was on the throne, your father was well favored. He was given money and lands beyond most of our—well, you know how vast and lovely your father's land is."

"Yes," Cecily said, feeling very stupid. She had never wondered where these things came from. She had merely assumed that there had always been plenty and there would always be plenty.

"But after the Prince was born, your father fell out of favor. The King would no longer see him."

"Why?" Cecily asked.

"As if I know!" The woman laughed. "He really has kept you in another world up there!"

Later, she went to a large bed chamber and changed into a pale shift that was still, somehow, darker than her skin. She stared at her arms, looking at the tracery of purple veins, mapping a geography of paths she might take, a maze of choices she did not know her way out of.

"You look cold," Vance said. "I could warm you."

Cecily thought that was a kind thing to say, as though he was more interested in her well-being than in her vermillion-painted mouth or the sapphires sparkling on her fingers. She didn't have the heart to stop him from taking her hand and pressing his lips to her throat. Lying beside his cold body afterward reminded her of sleeping with her sisters before they were only shades. The chill touch of his skin comforted her.

In the morning, the whole house wept with his sudden death.

Alice and Mirabelle wept, too, because although he was dead, he did not live on as they did. They could not catch his spirit as he passed.

She rode in a fast coach with her father and Liam was dead before word reached the household of Vance's burial. The second boy was much easier than she expected. At this wedding, her name had been Alice. In their bedchamber, he'd barely spoken; only torn off her gown and died. There was no time to steal out to the gardens. No time to bury her sisters.

Cecily's father was so pleased he could barely sit still as they pressed on to the palace. He ate an entire box of sweetmeats, chuckling to himself as he watched the landscape fly by.

He had brought something for her to eat, too, a familiar mix of herbs that she left sitting in their bowl.

"I don't want them," she said. "They make me sick."

"Just eat!" he told her. "For once, just do as you are bid."

She thought about throwing the bowl out of the window and scattering the herbs, but the smell of them reminded her of Mirabelle and Alice, who barely smelled like anything now. Besides, there was nothing else. Cecily ate the herbs.

She could still taste them in her mouth when the carriage arrived at the palace. She half expected to be clapped in irons and as she passed whispering courtiers, Cecily thought that each one was telling the other a list of her evil deeds.

We first met in the library. I was tall and plain, with pock-marked skin. Yes, I'm the prince in this story. Did you guess, Paul? Cecily later told me that when I first smiled at her, I still appeared to be frowning. What I remember was that she had the blackest eyes I had ever seen.

"This is your betrothed, Cecily," Cecily's father told me.

"I know who she is," I said. She looked very like the picture I had been given. Most girls don't. Your mother certainly didn't.

That afternoon, Cecily washed the dirt of the road off her clothing and went to walk in the gardens of the palace while her father made the final arrangements. The gardens were lush and lovely, more beautiful, even, than those of her father. Plants with heads full of seeds, large as the skulls of infants, lolled from thick stems. She touched the vivid purple and red fronds of one and it seemed to twitch under her fingers. The lacy foliage of another seemed like the parsley plant of her salad. Crushing it produced a pungent, familiar scent. It was like the breath of her sisters. She bent low for a taste.

"Stop! That's poisonous!" A gardener jogged down the path, wearing steel and leather gloves like those that belonged to her father. He had hair that flopped over his eyes and that he brushed back impatiently. "You're not supposed to be in this part of the garden."

"I'm sorry," Cecily stammered. "But what are these? I have them in my garden at home."

He snorted. "That isn't very likely. They're hybrids. There are no others like them in all the world."

She thought of the woman at her wedding telling how her father had once been close to the king. He must have taken cuttings from these very plants.

She began walking, hoping she might leave the gardener behind and be about her burying business. He seemed to misconstrue her wishes, however, pacing alongside her and pointing out prize blooms. She finally managed to put off a lengthy explanation of why the royal apples were the sweetest in the world by pretending a chill and retreating into the palace.

That night there was a feast in Cecily's honor. She sat at a long table set with crisp linens and covered with dishes she was unfamiliar with. There was eel with savory; tiny birds stuffed with berries and herbs, their bones crunching between Cecily's teeth; pears stuffed into almond tarts and soaked in wine; even a sugar-coated pastry in the shape of the palace itself, studded with flecks of gold.

"Oh," Mirabelle gasped. "It is all so lovely."

But Cecily realized that no matter how lovely, it disgusted her to bring the food to her mouth. She looked across the table and saw her father in deep conversation with the king, not at all behaving as though he was out of favor.

Later, Cecily left her room and went out to the garden. Her walk with the gardener had revealed where he kept his tools and she stole a spade. With her sisters fluttering around her, Cecily looked for the right spot for them to rest. In the moonlight, all the plants were the same, their glossy leaves merely silvery and their flowers shut tight as gates.

"Be careful," Mirabelle said. "You're the only one of us left."

"Whose fault is that?" Cecily demanded.

Neither of them said anything more as Cecily finally chose a place and began to dig. The rich soil parted easily.

That was what I saw her doing as I walked out of the palace. I had been looking for her, but when I found her, digging in the dirt, I didn't know what to say.

She saw me standing there and crouched. Her fingers were

black with earth and she looked feral in the dim light of the palace windows. I don't think she knew it, but I was afraid.

"Please," Cecily said. "I have to finish. I am digging a grave for my sisters."

I thought she was mad then, I admit it. I turned to go back to the house and get the guards, thinking that my plans were in shambles.

"Please," she said again. "I will tell you a secret."

"That you have come to kill me?" I asked her. "Like you killed Vance and Liam?"

She frowned.

It was then that I told her the part of her story she did not know and she told most of what I have said tonight. I will summarize for you, Paul. I know how tedious you find this sort of thing.

When he was a prince like yourself, my father had hired hers to kill those before him in line to the throne. He was very efficient; no one doubted but they had merely fallen ill. Mother told me this much before her death and I told it to Cecily.

Apparently, it was my birth that made Father send Cecily's father to the country. It made him uncomfortable to look at his own son and to consider the sort of son he had once been.

As I got older, however, he grew increasingly certain I was planning his death. He wrote to Cecily's father and coaxed him from retirement. Her father had a price, of course—Liam and Vance—some grudge avenged. I have forgotten the details. It doesn't matter. Our engagements were arranged.

"How did you find out?" Cecily asked when I finished speaking.

"My mother taught me to go through Father's correspondence." I had not expected her to be both the poison and the poisoner, and I found myself studying her pale skin and black eyes for some sign that it was true. I leaned toward her unconsciously and something about her smell, sweet as rot, made me dizzy. I stepped back abruptly.

"I will make this bargain with you," I said. It was not the bargain I had planned to make, but I tried to speak with confidence. "Kill my father and yours and you may bury your sisters in this garden. I will keep them safe for as long as I shall reign, and I shall make a proclamation so that the garden remains when I am no more."

She looked at me and I couldn't tell what she was seeing. "Will you bury me here as well?"

I stammered, trying to come up with an answer. She was smarter than I had given her credit for. Of course, she would be caught and slain. Men were coming now from the baronies, I was sure, to avenge the murders of her two husbands.

"I will," I said.

She smiled shyly, but her eyes shone. "And will you tend my grave and the graves of my sisters? Will you bring us flowers and tell us stories?"

I said I would.

Cecily finished the graves for Mirabelle and for Alice. Each girl curled up at the bottom of the pits like pale whorls of fog and Cecily buried them with her hands.

I wished that she was a normal girl, that I might have taken her hand or pulled her to me to comfort her, but instead I left the garden, chased by my own cowardice.

The next day, she put on her wedding gown, long white gloves, and dressed her own hair. At the wedding, she was called Cecily, and she promised to be my good and faithful wife. And she was. The best and most faithful of all my wives.

There was a feast with many toasts, one after the next. The king's face was red with drinking and laughter, but he would not look at me, even when he drank to my health. As a dish of almond tarts was passed, Cecily rose and lifted her own glass. She walked to where her father and the King sat together.

"I want to toast," she said and the assembled company fell silent. It is not the normal way of things for a bride to speak.

"I would thank my father, who made me, and the King, who also had a hand in my making." With those words, she leaned down and took her father's face in her hands and pressed her lips to his. He struggled, but her grip was surprisingly firm. I wondered what her mouth felt like.

"Farewell, Father," she said. He fell back upon his chair, choking. She laughed, not with mirth or even mockery, but something that was closer to a sob. "You crafted me so sharp, I cut even myself."

The King looked puzzled as she turned and took his hand in hers. He must have been very drunk, now that he thought himself safe from me. Certainly he wore no gloves. He pulled his fingers free with such force that he knocked over his wine. The pinkish tide spread across the white tablecloth as he died.

They shot her, of course. The guards. Eventually she even fell.

Yes, I suppose I embellished the story in places and perhaps I was a little dramatic, but that hardly matters. What does matter is that after they shot her I had her carried out to the garden—carefully, ever so carefully—and buried beside her sisters.

From each grave bloomed a plant covered in thorns, with petals like velvet. Its flowers are quite poisonous, too, but you already know that. Yes, the very plant you tried to poison me with. I knew its scent well—acrid and heavy—too well not to notice it in this golden cup you gave me, even mixed with cider.

In a few minutes the servants will come and unbind you. Surprised? Ah, well, a father ought to have a few surprises for his only son. You will make a fine king, Paul. And for myself, I will take this beautiful goblet, bring it to my lips and drink. Talking as much as I have makes me thirsty.

I have left instructions as to where I would like to be buried. No, not near your mother, as much as I was occasionally fond of her. Beside the flowers in the west garden. You know the ones.

Perhaps I should take the gag from your mouth so that you might protest your innocence, exclaim your disbelief, tell your father goodbye. But I do not think I will. I find I rather appreciate the silence.

Acknowledgments

Holly would like to thank Steve Berman, Kelly Link, and Cassandra Clare for reading and commenting on the stories. She would also like to thank the editors of the anthologies in which they originally appeared. Lastly, she'd like to thank Kelly and Gavin for their encouragement and enthusiasm in putting together this book.

Publication History

"The Coldest Girl in Coldtown" (*Eternal Kiss,* 2009)
"A Reversal of Fortune" (*The Coyote Road,* 2007)
"The Boy Who Cried Wolf" (*Troll's Eye View,* 2009)
"The Night Market" (*The Faery Reel,* 2004)
"The Dog King" appears here for the first time.
"Virgin" (*Magic in the Mirrorstone,* 2008)
"In Vodka Veritas" (*21 Proms,* 2007)
"The Coat of Stars" (*So Fey,* 2007)
"Paper Cuts Scissors" (*Realms of Fantasy,* 2007)
"Going Ironside" (*Endicott Journal of Mythic Arts,* 2007)
"The Land of Heart's Desire" appears here for the first time.
"The Poison Eaters" (*The Restless Dead,* 2007)

Holly Black (blackholly.com) is a bestselling author of contemporary fantasy. Some of her titles include *Tithe, Valiant* (winner of the Andre Norton Award), *Ironside,* the Spiderwick Chronicles (with Tony DiTerlizzi), and the graphic novel series The Good Neighbors (with Ted Naifeh). She lives in Amherst, MA, with artist Theo Black in a house with a secret library. She is currently working on a new series, The Curse Workers, which begins this spring with *White Cat.*